Antonia!
We've known eac[h]
I'm a writer! Enjoy the emotional weather f...
Liquid Sunshine
J.C.H—
08/15

Keep singing!! Much love

Liquid Sunshine

A Story About Love, Life, and Finding the Will of God

A Novel

Justin C. Hart

authorHOUSE®

AuthorHouse™
1663 Liberty Drive, Suite 200
Bloomington, IN 47403
www.authorhouse.com
Phone: 1-800-839-8640

First published by AuthorHouse 5/21/2009

ISBN: 978-1-4343-7088-4 (sc)
ISBN: 978-1-4343-7089-1 (hc)

Printed in the United States of America
Bloomington, Indiana

This book is printed on acid-free paper.

Unless otherwise noted, Scripture quotations are from the King James Version, Copyright 1979, 1980, 1982, 1990.

Scripture quotations marked NLT are taken from the Holy Bible, New Living Translation, copyright 1996, 2004. Used by permission of Tyndale House Publishers, Inc., Wheaton, Illinois 60189. All rights reserved.

Printed in the United States

Liquid Sunshine is a work of fiction. Any references to real people, events, establishments, organizations, or locales are intended only to give the fiction a sense of reality and authenticity. Other names, characters, and incidents are either a product of the author's imagination or are used fictitiously, as are those fictionalized events and incidents that involve real persons.

~ Dedication ~

With an overflowing amount of appreciation and gratitude, I dedicate this achievement to God and every God-given individual who has been a lamp unto my feet and a light unto my path. I sincerely thank you for helping me finish this painting to its fullest completion.

1 Corinthians 2:9 (NLT)

"No eye has seen, no ear has heard, and no mind has imagined what God has prepared for those who love him."

Romans 8:28 (NLT)

"And we know that God causes everything to work together for the good of those who love God and are called according to his purpose…"

Jeremiah 29:11(KJV)

"For I know the thoughts that I think toward you," saith the LORD, "thoughts of peace, and not of evil, to give you an expected end."

~Contents~

~ Preface: Emotional Weather ~

The voice of soft, drizzling raindrops tapping against your bedroom window late in the evening can be such a soothing and calming sound when the mood is just right, right? The same goes for the sound of crackling rain against your car windshield when you're parked, waiting patiently for a passenger to return. Have you ever waited in the rain? Depending on your state of mind right now, you can perceive rain as being a quiet shower of peace. But what happens when the rain never leaves you? What happens when your life becomes filled with rainy days? Will you remain indoors just to stay protected, or will you face the rain head-on and press forward to where you have to go? Are you the kind of person who allows the rain to control your moods, thoughts, and decisions? I'm not speaking of physical weather, but emotional weather. This is the type of weather that builds godly or ungodly characteristics deep in our souls.

The title *Liquid Sunshine* is a symbolic expression derived from simply taking the trials throughout life (rain) and merely perceiving them as growth from the Lord (sunshine). Understand this is the reason why sunshine and rain, good days and bad ones, have been given to us from God—so we can grow in moderation as plants do, trusting in him.

In this story of love, life, and finding the will of God, Jayden Rockaway, a charming senior in college, struggles to maintain a healthy relationship with the Lord, while involved with his girlfriend and an unwanted third party. After multiple breakups and much tension between the three of them, the Lord's will for his life is found.

Throughout this challenging experience, God paints a beautiful work of art and only by Jayden's willingness was it created. Once he stopped chasing the temporary and meaningless things of this world and pursued the perpetual and everlasting things that God wanted for him, he mentally saw a completed image, what many call *the big picture,* right before his very eyes. Now, we can all agree that hindsight is a wonderful explosion of revelation; however, to receive a glimpse of a painting before it is finished is a gift like none other.

Step into this story and share my umbrella, if you will. See how the good and bad weather of a particular season can blend together and create one beautiful day.

LIQUID SUNSHINE written by Justin C. Hart

It's raining / It's pouring/ It's coming down hard
Where's my umbrella when I need it?
It's coming down hard
These raindrops got kinetic energy and I think they're leaving scars
The Weatherman said a slight chance of rain
I wasn't prepared for this
Where's the sunshine when I need it?
I want these dark clouds dismissed
I feel like I'm the only one getting rained on at times
At times the rain is the only thing I feel
No more bad weather wounds
I need the sunshine to heal
Tomorrow's forecast: seventy-eight degrees, cool breeze, no clouds
That right there is enough to get me out the house
My clothes are still wet from the last few rainy days
I'll stand in the sun long enough for the liquid to fly away
Rejuvenate me/ Breathe life back into these bones
As much as I love good weather, the rain never leaves me alone
My umbrella is up, even in my home
I want to bask in the sun without a worry of rain
I love the fact that both are controlled by One and I know His name
I have a relationship with I AM
And I am not ashamed
He asked me if I was thankful for the weather, the test
I put my umbrella away and answered Him, yes
I have a testimony now and I feel extremely blessed
It's amazing how the rain and sun can build our character
Who can be mad at God for being so, so clever?

Liquid Sunshine

~ Conversations ~

1

What does this fall semester have in store for me? I asked myself at 9:15 a.m., moving slowly through the Hampton Roads Bridge Tunnel, excited. My anticipation of the first day of my seventh semester in college resembled that of a young child going to school for the first time. Thoughts of the unexpected breezed through my mind as I eventually arrived onto the urban campus of New Norfolk University.

The moment I stepped on campus ground, I lifted my hands to the cloudless, blue sky and took a deep breath of the fresh August air, ready to go through the motions of repetition. Like previous semesters, my college days were set up like clockwork, a circle—a cycle, to be exact. Being the smooth senior I was, my first morning was spent strutting through the halls of the Technology Building like I owned the place, chatting with classmates of old. Soon after, I stood in my advisor's office and waited in line to receive my pre-registered class schedule. I reviewed my arrangement and organized my free time around my new schedule, making it a daily routine.

One hot afternoon, during an hour break between classes, I made my way to my second home, also known as the library. To me, the library was more than just a large building created for studying and reading. It was more than an information site. It became my first and last option for sleep, socializing, and above all, a place to waste time. That day, on the familiar second floor of the library, I sat alone at a table for four and skimmed through my notes. It was only the second week of school, so my concentration wasn't on my work yet, but on any pretty feet that caught my attention. Because of the lack of traffic, my eyes continued to stretch themselves to my immediate right. The table to my right was perpendicular to mine and rested about 30-feet away. I knew who was sitting there. It was her! It was the same attractive girl that I had been secretly crushing from a year before, sitting alone at her table. My eyes couldn't help themselves. She knew that I was looking, and I obviously knew that she was looking back.

After playing eye games with one another, she broke my daze. She arose from her table and wandered my way. She had the features of a beautiful black and Venezuelan mix. Her exotic appearance was perfection to the natural eye. Her long legs and lengthy, dark hair ruffled my righteousness. She had hips for days and nice pants for weeks. She carried herself very well, full of poise and self-assurance. She was all that and a set of spinning rims! Show-stopping. Clearly, she was out of my league. Startled, I dropped my head and pretended like I didn't see her coming.

"Excuse me," she said with a sweet Spanish accent. "Can you help me with the copy machine?"

In an anxious yet relaxed manner, I raised my eyes and grinned. "Do you really need help with the copier?"

"Yep. I need to make two copies of these worksheets," her lips replied. "See?" She waved the pages back and forth. "Don't make fun of me. I need help with the machine."

"I'm not making fun of you," I said playfully, sliding back from the table. "How can I help?"

While I assisted her, my tail wagged like a puppy. I couldn't believe she chose me to help her. Of all people—me! After printing the second copy we returned to our tables. "Hey, can you keep me company?" she projected, seconds later from her chair. "We shouldn't sit alone, you know."

"Umm, yeah. Yeah," I shouted back, still a little jumpy. "Let me grab my things."

I was nobody's fool; I wasn't born yesterday. I promptly grabbed my books and sat across from her at her table, hiding my nervous hands. Immediately, we indulged in an informative exchange of words. We covered all the basics: hometown, birthday, family, and major. In the middle of our conversation, I glanced at my watch.

"Whoa! Hey, I gotta go," I said, standing up. "I gotta three o'clock class, and even if I hurry, I'll be late. Sorry I gotta run like this. My professor's known for locking students out. But, it was nice chatting with you though, Lydea."

She sat there and nibbled on her manicured thumbnail, watching me clumsily walk away, fumbling my textbooks. "You know what, Jayden?" She leaned forward. "Red Polo shirts make you look really handsome."

I paused. "Oh *reeeally?*" I bounced back to the table with charm. "Well, thank you. And if girls could be labeled handsome, you *most certainly* would be too. But since I can't call you handsome, I'll just say you're extremely fine, fine, beautiful, and fine. Did I mention fine?" I said, counting my fingers, giving her a wink and a full smile. She blushed as I returned my books to the table. "Let me get your number so we can keep in touch. I'm sure we can hold an even better conversation over the phone. You think so?"

"I think so," my striking new friend answered with her dimples showing. "I was hoping you'd ask for it. It's a New Jersey number. Is that all right?"

"That's not a problem at all. I'm ready. Go ahead."

Whether her number was local or long distance, I had just received the digits from the same beauty who I thought was completely out of my league. What an accomplishment! I was now the man! I jogged off to class with my mind going bananas.

Who can brag more—the guy who gets the most girls or the one who gets the best-looking girl? What were the chances of an average, clean-cut guy like myself retrieving the digits from a hottie like her? I bragged to my friends as if I'd never gotten a girl's number before. Why was I such a braggart? What did I do that was so unique and impressive? Pretty girls should be just that—pretty girls—right?

Well this pretty girl was different. She grabbed my thoughts daily. I didn't want her to think I was interested at first, so I refrained from calling. For days I didn't see her on campus, until one warm evening while watching a live game of intramural flag football from my car, I spotted her in the distance approaching the library. With quickness, I fled from my car and stood in between her and the library doors.

"Ms. Mireina," I called.

"Hey, Jayden," Lydea said, approaching with a grin. "It's good to see you again. How's your day going?"

"Great. I'm just enjoying this sexy weather. How about you?"

"Wait. Did you just call the weather sexy?"

"Uhhhh…yeah. What's wrong with that?" I asked.

"The weather can't be sexy. That's unheard of."

"Ah." I raised my finger to make a point. "If folks can call the weather beautiful on a nice day, then I can call it sexy on a *really* nice day. Look up. Say it ain't sexy."

Lydea looked up to the clear sky. "Okay. I'll admit. It is quite sexy today." She laughed.

"That's right." I laughed with her. "Don't steal my phrase either, girl."

We stood and spoke for a long while and not once did my legs get weary. There was more to this girl than just a set of starry eyes and an hourglass figure. She was a conversationalist just like myself, and right where I stood, I was sprung.

By the middle of the following month, I began walking Lydea to class. Her classmates often wondered if we were a couple; we'd chuckle and respond, "We're just friends." Even her aged English professor flattered us with a few compliments. She was like a trophy on my arm. I covered myself in pride when we walked together.

One morning before her class, the two of us posted-up in the crowded hallway and waited for her professor to arrive. "Jayden, you won't believe this," Lydea shared. "This past weekend, my best friend, Jason, asked to borrow my Maxima, talking about, *he needs* to go back to West Philly."

"Hold up." I turned to face her. "I thought you said he's driving his mama's Cadillac."

"He is, but remember last Wednesday during Hurricane Isabel when that tree branch shattered the windshield? I told you, didn't I? We were on the phone when Jason and I watched it happen from his sister's house."

"Yeah, yeah, yeah. I remember now. That was crazy."

"Tell me about it. Sooo, with me being the generous friend that I am, I gave him my car. Then the boy calls me later *the same night*, and guess what he said?"

"What? I hope he didn't crash it."

"Yes, he did." Lydea motioned with a mad face. "Jason told me that he nodded off while he was on the interstate and jacked up my entire driver's side."

"Dang, that's messed up," I empathized, curiously looking forward to meeting this privileged friend of hers.

"Tell me about it. It's still at a body shop in Philly getting fixed, so who knows when I'll get it back. Soon, I hope. I'll ask him when I see him later on today."

"Well, the sooner the better." I patted her shoulder.

"Yeah, we'll see. But, hey, my professor's coming down the hall with his elbow patches and bifocals," Lydea ridiculed. "Let me slide into class. Call me later, okay?"

"Aight, I got you. Try not to fall asleep today."

"Whatever, boy." She smiled. "Call me later."

By late afternoon, during our school's football pep rally, Lydea and I joined the large crowd of students outside of the Union Building on the open grass as the DJ pumped 50 Cent's hit single, "21 Questions."

"Hey, I see my best friend," she hollered, spotting Jason amongst the multitude of faces. Instantly, she led me by my hand to where he stood. They greeted with a tight hug. Within seconds she turned around and cheerfully introduced the both of us, standing next to him. "Jas, meet my new friend. This is Jayden Rockaway. Jayden, this is my best friend, Jason Steele. There, now the two of you are friends. I hope I don't mess up your names." She smirked at the irony. "Jayden, Jason. Jason, Jayden."

He puffed on a fresh cigarette with his Phillies baseball cap slightly tilted as he stood there, giving off an unfriendly vibe. His thick stature and trimmed beard made him look much older than what he probably was. *How does a guy like this become best friends with a girl like her?* I wondered, standing a few inches under him. We nodded out of respect towards one another and bumped fists. I stepped back and listened to the two of them converse while the hip-hop music moved the crowd. Waiting for her to return to me, I began feeling a little awkward as they laughed. I knew I had no influence over any of her male friends, so I didn't let it bother me. So what if she had friends of the opposite sex? I'm sure I had more than her. I'd be a fool to feel jealous this early in our companionship. We had no status. Nevertheless, I wanted one.

October had arrived and despite Jason being in the picture, Lydea's flirting towards me had become obvious. "You know what, Jayden? I have a crush on this one guy who goes here," she hinted sitting next to me in the library, stealing the wide rubber band from my wrist, "but I don't think he knows it."

"You don't think so?" I played along, hearing the same engaging line for several straight days.

"Nope. And he drives this nice, gold Honda Accord to school everyday. Do you think he'd like a girl like me?"

"Good question," I replied with a beaming smile, pretending the guy wasn't me. "He probably would. Have you asked him? He might like you too. You never know."

"No, not yet. He gives me butterflies," she continued to role-play. "But, I'll ask him the next time I see him by his car. I'll tell you what he says, okay?"

"Yeah. Let me know. Make sure you tell me."

I couldn't believe it. The same girl that I had been sweating for three full semesters was before me each day, claiming to have a secret crush also. It wasn't long before I took my situation before the Lord God Almighty, and he gave me an answer that I ran with. At the appropriate moment, I asked Lydea to be my girl, and she concurred in her beautiful language, "*Claro que quiero ser tu novia, Jayden!*"

7

Breakdown

Although the two of us had spent countless hours in each other's presence, and had spoken for numerous hours over the phone, I still felt somewhat pressured. Even after receiving an answer from God, an uneasy gut feeling kept me double minded. I reasoned with myself, thinking, *Well, we vibe very well together. I like her a lot, and from what she tells me, she likes me too. Plus, the girl is stunning. What am I waiting for? Lord, talk to me. I need to hear you speak.*

On that special day when Lydea became my first official college girlfriend, my mind spoke through my mouth, but my heart remained quiet. I had no clue how it felt about this decision. All I knew was that if I didn't snatch her up, then some lucky guy would have. With high expectations, I put my bachelor days behind me in a pursuit of love. Oh, the joy and pain of love.

~ A Crooked Thumbs-Up ~

2

I will never forget the night I received my answer from the Lord. My prayer was simple. While resting in my bed with the lights off, I gazed at the slow moving ceiling fan and repeated, "God, is she the one? Lord, is she good for me? Jesus, do you approve of Lydea?" In the middle of my midnight prayer, laying there, my eyes gently closed. My thoughts began to drift. I envisioned the upright thumb of Jesus moving in a meter-like motion, swaying left to right. It gradually leaned to the side and continued downward. Then it quickly sprung up, just to return downward again. His thumb then began moving extremely fast. It was as if God wasn't giving me a definite approval. However, a tilted upright position was seen throughout most of this vision, so I perceived it as my answer. Still half asleep, I thanked the Lord for his confirmation, or what I thought was confirmation. Seconds later, the Lord spoke to my conscience, saying, *I want you to show her how a Christian is supposed to be. Introduce Lydea to me and edify her character.* The Lord's commandment settled in my thoughts.

Two months prior, while completing a summer internship in Atlanta, I incurred a spiritual growth-spurt and was baptized at my Uncle Isles' small church. So, being the on-fire churchgoer that I was, I was motivated to live up to God's commandment. I was a new person through Christ and my past was no longer a part of me. Though I lacked much biblical knowledge and evangelical skills, my walk with the Lord was fairly good at the time. I prayed for sensitive ears to hear his voice and I received exactly that.

Weeks into my new relationship, the weather was lovely. I thought my decision to claim Lydea as my girl was the best choice of the semester—until late one evening, sitting on the second floor of the library our textbooks were pushed aside and we transitioned into an imperative discussion that could not have been covered up any longer. Everything changed once she came clean.

"Jayden, I need to inform you of a few things that took place during the storm last month."

"All right," I responded, bent over tying my shoelaces. "What's up?"

"You remember the girl from my Ethics class who invited me to stay with her until school opened back up?"

"Yeah, I guess."

"Look at me," she said, pulling my shoulder back. "This is serious. I lied about her being a girl. It was actually a guy from my class. I was only at his place for a few hours. He's a complete slob. Plus he kept telling me how pretty I was, which totally creeped me out. So, I knew that I wasn't gonna stay the whole night. I hated the feeling he gave me," she said, shaking it off. "That's the real reason why I ended up staying with Jason and his sister."

My emotionless face disguised my displeasure.

"Jay, I'm sorry I didn't tell you earlier," Lydea apologized, continuing with her confessions. "And you also need to know that I didn't sleep on the floor at their townhouse like I told you. I actually slept in the same bed with him, but nothing happened," she fervently made clear, in a broken voice. "It was nothing like that. He didn't want me sleeping on the couch, that's all. I'm sorry I lied about that too."

Hearing the truth made my heart sink deeper into the pit of disappointment. I looked away in anger. I had heard enough. I shut my textbook and kept my mouth under control. I began packing my things and Lydea did the same.

"Jay, are you okay?" she asked.

"I'm good," I replied in a subtle tone. I stood up from the table, struggling to get my textbook into my bag, which was already filled with two large binders. Soon after, we walked down the stairs and yielded at the sliding exit doors with several students, watching the rain fall from the night's sky. Despite the weather, I pressed through the huddle with no protection. I headed to my car and Lydea followed. Our clothes were saturated within seconds. Once we hit the main strip of campus, I stopped by a lamppost. A feeling of letting go came over me. Tears of disappointment built up in my eyes. I hung my head and mumbled, "Good night, Lydea. I'm sorry it didn't work out."

"Huh? I didn't hear you." She lifted my chin. "Did you say something?"

"I said, 'I'm sorry it didn't work out,'" I repeated.

She stared with confusion. "What are you talking about? What does that mean?"

The rain grew stronger. I ignored her words and side stepped her presence. Lydea grabbed my shoulder and turned me around with strength. Looking into my fractured face, she yelled, "Jayden, what do you mean, you're sorry it didn't work out? Was it something I said? We were just friends when all that happened. You know that," she explained. "What else do you want me to say? I'm trying to be honest. I'm sorry."

The rain blended in with my watery eyes. My temper was still thumping inside of me. "I can't do it," I grunted, clenching my fists, looking at her soiled face.

"Why?" she questioned, flailing her arms. I stood in silence, unable to justify. "Why, Jayden? Speak!"

We were both completely drenched by this time. I sidestepped her again, trucking my way through the parking lot in the cold rain. She tugged on my forearm. I paced faster. She eventually faded behind me. I got inside my car and couldn't control my tears. My expectations of Lydea smacked hard against the pavement. I literally sobbed with volume, asking God, "Why?"

Not a minute after I sat down in my driver's seat, I heard tapping on my window. It was her. Why did she have to come back? I wanted to be left alone. Regardless of the hurt and pain, I opened the door and let her in. She sat across my lap and held me as the weather and I both cried.

Breakdown

The inner soreness that disappointment can bring forth is one of the most painful emotions to feel. I don't know why I broke down so easily that night. I wanted this girl to be perfect. I didn't want to find any flaws in her. My previous relationship had been filled with drama and I didn't want this one to be its sequel. Why did I feel so disappointed? Were my expectations of this girl too high? When she came clean about her lies, it was extremely hard for me to swallow. Never mind the fact that she actually slept in the same bed as Jason. Her spoken words in the library were what I called an *honest surprise*—being told something that is truthful, yet heartbreaking. This episode was the first crack in our relationship and it wouldn't be the last.

Picture the scene: a couple standing under a glowing street lamp in the rain, late at night, soaking wet, and breaking up. What a sight! A movie producer couldn't have created a more intense clip. I wish I had been acting. The built-up bitterness from past relationships showed through my red eyes as I drove home. I prayed for answers from God that night and asked him to restore my brokenness. I was restored, but I received no answers.

~ I Won't Get Mad ~

3

The very next day at school, I followed my daily schedule and made no effort in contacting Lydea. Leaving my night class, I felt the vibration of my phone in my pocket.

"Hey, Jay," she voiced. "I'm standing by your car. Are you leaving soon?"

"Yeah. I'm done for the night," I answered. "Why?"

"Oh, it's nothing. I just wanted to chat. I'll see you when you get here, okay?"

"Aight," I said hesitantly. "Give me a few minutes, though. I just left class."

"All right. I'll be right here."

I walked along the sidewalk minutes later and spotted Lydea resting on the hood of my car, texting a message.

"Hey!" I shook her from behind.

"Ahh!" she shrieked, dropping her phone. "You scared the crap outta me. Don't do that, boy! Look what you made me do."

"My bad. You knew I was coming."

"So?" She bent down to pick it up. "Next time, make more noise. Ugh. You know this campus is *loco*."

"Yeah, yeah, yeah. Good to see you too," I said, sucking my teeth, placing my bag in the trunk of my car. "Are you coming from the library?"

"No, not exactly," she slowly responded.

"Sooo, you're coming from your room?" I pried.

"Well, not really. Jason met me earlier and we walked around campus for a little while," she admitted. "Oh yeah, and your little freshman friend, Chelsea, left another note on your windshield."

"Yo, I told that girl to chill with these notes," I said, grabbing the paper from Lydea's grasp. "I'm gonna hav'ta tell Cassell about his lil' sister. This is ridiculous. What'd it say this time?"

"Read it and find out."

"Nah. You know what? It's not important," I said, tearing through it. "Chelsea doesn't listen very well. But, anyways, back to you. Where'd you and Jason go?"

"Not far," Lydea yawned, turning from me. "We walked by the, umm, Student Union Building and over by the teacher's parking lot." She pointed indirectly. "Nowhere really. Why?" she shot back, wondering why I cared.

"Oh, no reason," I replied leaning against my car. "I'm just curious."

"Listen, Jayden, if I tell you something, will you promise not to get mad?" she asked, stepping towards me.

"What are you talking about? It depends what it is," I said, meeting her halfway.

"Promise me that you won't get mad!" she pressed, reaching for my hand.

"Fine," I agreed, touching her fingers. "I won't get mad. *There.*"

After a long sigh, she looked me in the eyes and mumbled, "He kissed me."

My heart sank. I shook my head furiously. I covered my face with my hands and turned away. "What do you mean he kissed you, Lydea?" I raised my voice. "Where?"

"On my lips."

"What! Oh nah. I don't believe this." I circled my car to leave. "I'm gone."

"No, wait. Don't go. Hear me out," she insisted, circling my car also. "There are certain things I don't speak about often and Jason is one of them. If he wasn't in my life the way that he is, I'd be a complete wreck."

"If you expect me to stand here and listen to you justify what y'all did, then I'm done," I told her. "Forget that."

"Listen, I'm not justifying anything. You're my boyfriend. I'm taken. I know that. What he did was wrong, but he's my friend."

"What does that have to do with him kissing you?"

"Can I please talk? I'll get to that in a second. I'm telling you something that no one else knows about me. Will you listen?" she fired back. "Jason and I are friends, okay? Actually, we're best friends. And, unfortunately, I don't have too many people in my life that I consider a friend. I have Traci, my other best friend who used to go here, and Jason, whom you've already met. *You*, on the other hand, are my boyfriend. There's only one of you."

"So, what does that mean?"

"It means that I acknowledge Jason as my friend and you as my man. The problem is *he* doesn't see you as my man. He sees himself as my man, which he's not. And he knows he's not," she said as practicing band members sounded their trumpets in the distant air. "Jay, as crazy as it sounds, Jason has made himself a part of my life," she declared, pacing in front of me. "He's been my crutch. I mean, my father might as well be non-existent, so it's like Jason has taken his place. He even buys me things, expensive things. And I'm telling you all this because I think you should know. It's been very difficult to get rid of him."

"Thank you for telling me all that," I said with my patience wearing low. "Still, what does that have to do with him kissing you on your lips?"

"I told you already," she said frustrated. "Jason looks at me as *more* than his best friend, okay? That boy has wanted to be my man from the jump," she said, pulling her lip-gloss from her purse.

"So why don't y'all stop playin' games with each other and hook up then?" I asked with a straight face. "This way I can be gone."

"You ain't going anywhere." She waved her left hand. "I don't like that boy. I have absolutely no physical attraction to him, whatsoever. So stop stressing. Look at me," she said, standing before me, reaching for my face. "*Look.* You're the only one I want. Will you please forgive me?"

I stared into Lydea's eyes until my attention was taken by two loud gentlemen walking towards their nearby SUV. "You know, you make this really hard for me," I said with my lips tightened. "But, yes, I forgive you. Just don't let—"

"I know, I know," she said, quickly embracing me. "It won't happen again. I promise."

Breakdown

That night by the car, one of the most confusing conversations I can remember had taken place. My girl claimed to have had no feelings for Jason, yet the time they spent together made me think differently. She had even found a reason for his inappropriate actions. Were they a couple or not? Was I the clown in their circus being laughed at or was Lydea telling me the truth? My mind had no answers. Lydea had no answers. There were no answers for my ignorance. I was aware that the two of them had been friends well before I had come onto the scene, but what kind of friendship did they have? Even if she didn't look at him as anything more than a friend, this wasn't a normal platonic relationship, if there is such a thing. Ask yourself, if someone were to kiss your mate on the lips, would you consider that cheating? Could you forgive them?

When Lydea had asked for forgiveness, she looked me dead in my eyes. There was something about her eye contact that changed the meaning of her words. She could take the word love and explode it into a flood of emotions. Her eye contact could repair a broken heart into a whole one, and could deceive a mended heart even faster. Whether she was sincere or not, her pretty, light colored eyes made me feel like she was the victim. The more I examined Lydea and Jason's friendship, the greater my insecurities grew. I concluded that I had a serious situation at hand.

~ Masquerade of Fear ~

4

By the middle of the semester, my workload had become very heavy. Being involved in a side project with one of my close classmates named Graham (a comical, vertically challenged, chubby friend of mine, who everybody referred to as G), and working a part-time job at a pet store in my hometown of Newport News didn't make school any easier. With all that was going on, an unstable relationship was the last thing I wanted to deal with. Days had gone by and I still wasn't over the whole kissing incident. That Tuesday, I called Lydea after my three o'clock class and said those famous words: "We need to talk."

Shortly after we hung up, we met on the Greek Walk, a decorated circular concrete path covered with stylish graffiti that represented the fraternities and sororities on the yard. The weather was beautiful, but our moods were about to get ugly. We sat down on one of the wooden benches under a large tree and I spoke up.

"All right, Lyd…about us." I leaned forward and rested my elbows on my knees, rubbing my hands together, carefully gathering my thoughts. "I don't think I can do this anymore."

"Do what anymore?" She shrugged. "I don't understand."

"Me and you. This is our first time seeing each other *all* day. My classes are outta control; my job is wearing me out; plus, I'm hoping to get some extra money from this side project that me and G are working on. Honestly, my time is shot, girl. I don't have enough time to be your man. I can't do this relationship thing," I said, exhausted. "I just can't."

"So you're saying you want to breakup with me because you don't have enough time?" she questioned, with a facial expression that made me feel like I should've given her a better reason than the one I had. "Jayden, have I ever asked you for more of your time? Have I ever said that our time together is insufficient?" Lydea shifted her neck. "Huh?"

"No," I said, breathing hard, watching the autumn leaves fall to the ground.

"So why would you think that? I'm content with our time. Yes, I'd love to spend more time with you, but if this is all I can get for now, then I'll take it." The longer she defended our relationship, the more emotional she became.

"Well, then maybe it's me," I interrupted. "Maybe I feel like I'm not being the best boyfriend I can be. Yes, I want to be with you, more than you'll ever know. But guess what? I can't because my plate is full. I can't do this, Lyd."

"Why do you give up on me so easily?" she boldly asked, sitting there with her legs crossed. "Tell me the truth."

I had plenty of reasons to give her. Pick one, any one. Instantly, the words spilled off my tongue. "Oh, you want the truth, huh? I'll give you the truth," I said, correcting my posture. "Lydea, I'd give you every second of every hour if I could because I know that when we're not together, your boy is on his way. You want the truth? How about not bouncin' with him to get food every chance you get! You ain't gotta remind me that I can't afford you."

"What's that supposed to mean?" she sprang up.

"You know what? Never mind," I caught myself, remembering her dislike for cafeteria food.

"Don't bring Jason into this. I'm lucky he cares enough to not see me starve."

"Never mind," I repeated.

The reason for this breakup was clear to me. However, in the midst of us being parked on the bench, my breakup agility was slowly decreasing. My heart began to listen.

"Why are you doing this? What did I do wrong, Jayden?" she challenged. "Everyone who has ever cared about me has left me. My mom left me. My dad doesn't even speak to me. And now you? Please don't do this."

The sympathy I had for Lydea grew within me. I was blind to all manipulation. I still wanted to be her man—I really did. I wanted to be her hero. I wanted to be her lighthouse. I wanted to be her crutch. I wanted to be her answer. I wanted to be her life coach. I wanted to be her best friend. I wanted to be her lover. I wanted to be the shoulder she cried on. I wanted to be her everything. This was the same girl that I had desired for over a year. Was I really breaking up with her because of my lack of time? No, but that was my excuse. I was filled with reasons and excuses, and neither one prevailed.

Still seated, she advised how I could make better use of my time. It was like she transformed into a great saleswoman right before my eyes. While she attempted to sell me an item that I had no intention of buying again, a small voice from within said, *Introduce Lydea to me and edify her.* In an instant, I began to snicker.

"What's so funny?" she shouted.

"Boy, boy, boy. You're something else, you know that?" I stood to my feet, shaking my head, as she sat puzzled. "You could sell salt to a slug, couldn't

21

you?" I pulled Lydea to her feet and wrapped her tight in my arms. "I'm sorry for giving up on you," I whispered, releasing my long embrace.

"Do you mean it? 'Cause I don't want you here if you don't want to be," she said dabbing the corners of her eyes.

"Yes. I mean it. I'll do my best to be here for you. I'm sorry." I then planted a soft kiss on her cheek. "C'mon, don't let the sun catch you crying," I said with my arm around her waist, as we strolled off into the direction of her dorm. Once again, my emotions were knotted. I was longing for a relationship yet fearful of being hurt.

Edgar Lee Masters, the prolific author of Spoon River Anthology (Dover Publications), once wrote:

I HAVE studied many times
The marble that was chiseled for me—
A boat with a furled sail at rest in a harbor.
In truth it pictures not my destination
But my life.
For love was offered me, and I shrank from its disillusionment;
Sorrow knocked at my door, but I was afraid;
Ambition called me, but I dreaded the chances.
Yet all the while I hungered for meaning in my life.
And now I know that we must lift the sail
And catch the wind of destiny
Wherever they drive the boat.
To put meaning in one's life may end in madness,
But life without meaning is torture
Of restlessness and vague desire—
It is a boat longing for the sea and yet afraid.

Breakdown

Should fear be felt in a relationship? The kind of fear I'm talking about isn't the intimidating type or the reverence type, but the uncertainty type. I was uncertain about what to expect from Lydea. I was uncertain about what to anticipate if I actually fell in love with her. I wanted my decision of being with her to be a good choice, yet it wasn't looking too good.

If it weren't for the Lord speaking to my conscience after I broke off our relationship, I would've walked away. I was double minded from the beginning and dealing with her and Jason's friendship was nowhere in my plans. I'll admit; I was afraid. I was afraid of being disappointed again from another drama-filled relationship. I wanted to avoid the mere presence of drama, but I guess God had other plans for me. It's not often found in the Bible that God's chosen individuals are reminded by him to fulfill their purpose. However, in my case, regardless of my unwillingness, he reminded me and I took heed.

~ Autumn Daze ~

5

It had been irking me for weeks. I had to know where Lydea's head was in our relationship. I had to know where she and Jason stood in their friendship. I was willing to confront my foe. My curiosity forced me to speak to Jason face-to-face and squash this foolishness. So, late one evening, after several hours of my lady and I being stationed at our usual study spot, we agreed to meet him outside of her dormitory.

"You know I'm willing to get rid of him, right?" Lydea said.

"*Riiight*," I replied, unmoved, leaving the library.

"I'm serious. Just tell me. If Jason's messing up what we have together, then I'll let him go. It's that simple."

"Let him go?" I said, wondering why she needed to cut him off. "All I'm asking for is a line to be drawn so we can maintain a healthy relationship. If y'all can't adjust the rules to y'all's friendship, then we're in trouble," I explained, holding her hand while walking along the tree covered path.

We approached her dorm and I recognized Jason's smoky presence from far-off. I glanced at his appearance to compare it with mine and no feelings of jealousy arose. He gave me no reason to envy him. With Lydea standing close to me, the three of us made a triangle shape and waited to see who would start the discussion. I knew that the tongue was something that no man could tame, so my words were deliberately under control as I sparked the first question.

"Yo, what's up with you and Lydea's friendship, man?" I casually tossed at Jason. "How long y'all been friends?"

"For a while, I guess," he responded with his relaxed, Philadelphia demeanor. "A couple of years now, maybe."

"Have the two of you always been like this? You know, each other's shadow?" I pricked.

"*Each other's shadow?*" Jason echoed. "I ain't nobody's shadow. I like to kick it with her and she likes kickin' it with me. You gotta problem with that, dog?" he tested.

"Nah," I said calmly. "Problems need solutions. This ain't a problem."

My inquiry continued for several minutes, as I received nothing but shrugs from Lydea and short-lived responses from Jason. Consciously, I danced around the basis of our meeting. Without further delay, I built up my audacity. I stood with perfect posture and bombed away, "Yo, what were you thinking when you kissed my girl?"

He chuckled faintly, thrown off by my question. He straightened his cap and reached into his loose-fitting black leather jacket and lit another cigarette. Before he spoke one word, smoke polluted the air. "L, why's this dude asking me all these off-the-wall questions?" he said, taking another pull from the cigarette. "Hell if I know why I did it, I just did it. I couldn't help it. I mean, look at her."

"Wha-*what*! Are you serious?" I said in disbelief, glancing at Lydea fidgeting with her hair, and then looking back at Jason with a fuming glare. "You couldn't help it? I think you could've. I think it won't happen again, I'll tell you that."

"You think so?" Jason nodded.

"Yeah, I do."

Moments later, I realized I was standing there looking stupid in front of my girl. This was not what I had in mind when I planned for the three of us to meet. I had actually created a list of things to address, but my thoughts had gone blank. "You know what? I'm done," I told them. "It's too cold out here for us to be staring at each other and not saying anything. So I take it that all is understood, right?" They looked up at each other, giving no reply. "Yo, it's whatever. Just remember this," I aimed at my opposition, digging for respect, "I'm Lydea's man, and you're her friend. Period."

I took Lydea's hand and pulled her away towards her dormitory entrance. Jason chuckled under his breath again and stepped in the opposite direction. I couldn't understand why I needed to clarify the boundaries of a friendship between two grown college students. It opened my eyes to their maturity. It was definitely a ridiculous conversation to have, but it was much needed on my end.

Days rolled by and I saw less of Lydea's friend, causing our relationship to blossom. I was pleased in knowing that my courageous act was not done in vain. In her presence, I tried to keep our burdens light with laughter. My humorous side never went dry. I kept a funny story up my sleeve to keep her laughing with me. I'd bring up our dating days and it would quickly become a brisk walk down memory lane.

"Hey, you remember our first date?" I asked while we studied in the library, recalling the night at MacArthur Center Mall in Downtown Norfolk and how we had shared the same large appetizer. "You know, I really didn't know what to think of you. I remember *trying* to hold a conversation, but you were too busy stuffing your face," I said, making light of the moment. "Your mouth was so full, you couldn't even answer. It was so funny. Hand to mouth. Hand to mouth. I was like, *Dang, this girl can eat.*"

"Whatever, don't make fun of me now. You were the one that kept pushing food my way." Lydea laughed at herself. "I don't even wanna know what you thought of me. You probably thought I was a pig."

"A pig? Nah. A hungry college student maybe, but not a pig." I smiled. "Remember all that rain?"

"How could I forget? Buckets of water were more like it. I'm glad it eased up, though."

"Yeah, me too. It eased up *just* enough for me to take you to Old Dominion's hiding place. Their campus isn't far from ours, you know? We should try to go again."

"I didn't know *where* you were taking me." Lydea grinned. "Some dark dead-end road. I was praying you weren't some psycho."

"A psycho?" I said, lightly insulted. "That's my spot, girl. I wanted you to see the Elizabeth River from the pier."

"Yeah, I know. I'm only joking. It was beautiful," she praised. "It's wild, now that I'm thinking about it. I mean, our first date: sitting on a wet bench, on a misty night, learning about each other. The two of us simply sat and conversed like we had no other cares in the world."

"Most girls would've stayed in the car on a night like that," I shared with my arm around her shoulder. "But you, you're different—in a good way. I like that about you, Lyd."

"Awww. Thank you, Jay. You're different too."

"C'mon, you're just saying that."

"No, really. I'll admit, that night was truly exceptional, for a change. Guys don't usually have a plan on the first date. I think our opening engagement was perfect."

Perfect was exactly the way I would've described it also. When the two of us spoke with substance, it became impossible to bring our relationship down. We connected in every way. Our time together gave me confidence and countered my fluctuating insecurities, but I was falling too fast for this girl and I knew it. I felt it deep within.

Breakdown

Infatuation is so blinding in the early stages, is it not? I was interested in all that Lydea revealed, but I only saw what was in the physical realm. My interests were merely surface-based. Metaphorically, it's similar to a large iceberg protruding out of the arctic and revealing only its tip. Yet, if you view what's underneath the ocean's water level, you will find that the tip of the iceberg doesn't even compare with what is below. It will blow your mind! So much of Lydea was hidden from my eyes. I was actually falling for the tip of this beautiful girl, but I wasn't satisfied. I wanted to know all of her, from the smooth to the rough.

Lydea's personality and physical traits were extremely intriguing, yet what my heart really wanted was her character. Her personality reminded me of a blend between a street-smart Hilary Banks and a book-smart Jessica Simpson—clumsy yet cute, simple but funny. On the other hand, her character was something that I had to study. It wasn't as obvious as her personality. Regardless of what I knew or didn't know, let's call a spade a spade; I was going through the beginning stages of love. My feelings were fluttering. I was elated when we vibed without distractions. She was my girl and I was her man.

~ Secured Insecurity ~

6

The month of November was lively. A few weeks before the Thanksgiving holiday approached, the Lord directly spoke to my heart about writing my parents a letter on random issues, including their upcoming 25th wedding anniversary. The whole house was excited. My father was busy doing much planning, while my older brother, Reno, and I brainstormed with ideas. My mother and younger sister, Rachel, were the most eager to celebrate.

That weekend I shared with Lydea about my parents' anniversary and my plans to write them a long letter of encouragement and gratitude. Chatting over the phone, we both agreed on the impact of family values and how a loving mother and father combination in the home could positively affect a child growing up. We began sharing personal childhood memories, which motivated Lydea to write a letter to her father as well, a man who she acknowledged was becoming distant to her.

"You think this letter will bring me and my papa closer?" she asked with hope. "*I am* his only daughter."

"Yeah. You've got nothing to lose and everything to gain," I encouraged. "I'm sure you have a lot on your heart. Write about the things you're afraid to tell him. Let him know how you feel about his phone calls."

"The lack of is more like it," she said with her TV loud enough for me to hear *The Real World* actors arguing. "One phone call a semester is terrible. But, I mean, I'll try to share my feelings with him. It won't be easy. Plus, come January, he's getting married to a woman who he barely knows. So *you know* I got a lot to write about."

"Good. Write 'em a four page letter then. And when you're finished, I can edit it. You don't wanna give him some elementary literature, do you? We gotta look like scholars, Lyd!"

"Uhh, although English is my second language, I don't make mistakes when it comes to writing, unlike you. If you'd like, I'll gladly edit your letter though."

"Whatever, you nerd," I joked until it became late. "You were gonna edit mine anyways. So there."

Days later in the library, we took advantage of our idle time. Lydea typed my mom's letter and I handwrote the outline of my dad's. She clicked away as my hometown, high school friend, the university's star running back, walked up.

"Jay-Rockafella, what's up, fam?" Cassell asked, dapping me up with his strong grip. "You good?"

"Everything is everything, yo. Just staying busy," I said, tapping Lydea's left knee under the table.

"Hello Cassell," she said, rapidly typing. "I'm surprised to see *you* in the library. Shouldn't you be in the weight room getting your legs ready for this Saturday's spanking?"

31

"Hello to you too, L. I just left from there, stank you very much. Dog, get your girl," he nudged. "Whoa, stop the presses." Cassell paused. A girl we didn't recognize stood a short distance away at one of the research computers. "You see that?" he said lowly. At the same moment, our eyes burned a hole straight through the shorthaired foreigner in the tight outfit, slightly bent over.

"Nice pants!" I exclaimed under my breath.

"Jayden, who are you looking at?" my girlfriend said, still typing.

"Huh?" I promptly replied.

Lydea turned her head and spotted the same girl we were gawking at. A hard slap across my shoulder got my attention. "Stop!"

"What? I don't know that girl," I yelped, still looking in her direction, as if my lady wasn't sitting next to me.

"Will you stop it?" Lydea repeated, raising her voice an octave, still hitting me. "Stop staring at that girl's tail. That's so disrespectful. I'm typing this letter for *your* mother and you're checking out that hoochie's backside!"

"Okay. Okay. My bad, I'm sorry. Dang." My eyes went back to my outline. "I don't know who she is, that's all."

"Oh please," Lydea said with an attitude.

"Yo, Jay, I'm 'bouta introduce myself." Cassell cackled, patting his cornrows. "Hollatcha boy."

"Aight, dog." I turned back around. "My bad."

"Yeah, whatever," Lydea said, still upset.

"C'mon, gimme a break. Don't be trippin' like you're innocent. You've pulled worse stunts than that."

"Like what? Name one."

"Name one? I can name more than one." I twisted in my chair to face her. "The night we left from the basketball season opener against Virginia Union, you were getting off the phone with your boy and finished it off with an, 'All right. I love you too.' Now what kinda trash was that? I'm *still* mad about it. Let's talk about that right now."

"Jayden, I always tell my best friends that I love them when I say good-bye," she bounced back. "I tell Traci I love her all the time. You know that."

"Traci? Traci who?"

"Tall and slender Traci—my other best friend from my freshman and sophomore year. You haven't met her yet. She's at East Carolina. I talk about her all the time."

"Not to me, you don't. Either way, I don't wanna hear that mess anymore. There's a double standard, and those words are too heavy to just throw around like that."

I knew Lydea had mentioned Traci's name to me before. I got a better understanding when she told me how Jason, Graham, and a group of other guys used to kick it with the two of them their freshman year. Once she had become friends with Jason, the rest of the crew soon followed. They hung out on a regular basis, particularly Jason, Traci, and Lydea. However, being long time friends wasn't enough for her to win our argument. To hear my lady tell another guy, who wasn't family, that she loved him was definitely something I didn't care to hear again. Sadly enough, it wasn't the last time I heard it come out of her mouth. Days later, she repeated it.

"Yo, for real, out of respect for me, could you not say that to him again?" I requested. "No woman who has a man should say those words to another guy who's just a friend."

"I love him as a friend, Jay. Nothing more," she defended, stuffing her phone back in her purse.

"Well, prove it to me by not telling him anymore."

"Fine. Whatever you want. Let's just drop it."

That Saturday, as usual, I worked the register at the pet store, while a few cities away, Lydea was with her friend, Jason. I hated the two of them hanging out on the weekend, every weekend. He would usually transport her in his Cadillac to the nearest mall or shopping center. Wal-Mart and Target were her favorite mega stores. When they weren't shopping, they were at his sister's townhouse in Chesapeake, wasting time, washing clothes, and watching TV. This was the story that I was given when I questioned how her day went. Her words never changed. Over time, I learned to tolerate their weekends together, but I never once accepted them.

Sunday evening, after my shift was complete, I took a trip into Norfolk to pre-celebrate the good news of Lydea's academic honorary award within her major, criminal justice, that she was to receive on Monday.

"Hey, hot mama!" I said over the phone, animated, as I drove. "Where does my intelligent lady wanna go for dinner?"

"I don't know. What's open this late on a Sunday?"

"Good question. I couldn't tell you."

"Well, IHOP's always open. You wanna go there?" she suggested.

"IHOP it is. Give me like twelve minutes, aight? I'll meet you outside."

Soon after driving past the security gate on campus, I spotted her waiting by a lamppost along the sidewalk of her dorm.

"There's my girl!" I shouted out the side window, parking right in front of her. We greeted with a tight hug.

"I'm glad you came to see me tonight, babe," she said with a bright smile.

"No problem," I said holding the passenger door open. "I just wanted to be the first to celebrate with you, that's all."

Once we got to IHOP and sat down, we enjoyed pancakes, scrambled eggs, and laughter. Afterwards, we relived our first date by the water on Old Dominion University's campus. Sitting on the dock of the bay that night dissolved all worries of school, family, and our relationship. There's something special about being near a calm body of water, under a full moon at the stroke of midnight that can supernaturally melt the soul. We eventually returned to campus and I embraced my lady all the way back to her dorm, struggling to repel the cold autumn breeze.

We continued our conversation about the upcoming holiday as I drove home. "Jay, you don't understand," she said. "My only option right now for a decent Thanksgiving dinner and a place to stay is with Jason's family in Philadelphia."

"How did his family become your only option?" I asked, scorning the idea. "Call your folks and tell them when they can expect you."

"No. I can't just call them and tell them to expect me."

"Why not? Just call 'em," I pleaded, hoping she wouldn't leave with her warped friend. But no matter how hard I tried to persuade, there was nothing I could say or do.

"If my family wanted me home for Thanksgiving, they would've called me by now," Lydea added. "And you're gonna be in Atlanta anyways. You and your family are still going down there, right?"

"Yeah, but I'll be with my family. That's the difference. You know I don't trust that dude. I don't care if he is your friend. He ain't mine. You're making me throw my trust around, girl."

By the end of the month, my feelings were so unstable. The obstacle of insecurity stood in between us and frequently taunted my confidence. By

Thanksgiving Day, Lydea and I were separated by hundreds of miles. While my family stayed at my Aunt Cheryl's house, my mom's sister, Lydea stayed with Jason's family, his mother and siblings for the holiday. We talked often. Her voice brought a grin to my face, but that same grin was spun into a frown the morning I heard her say, "Jayden, I don't know what to do. He won't stop flirting."

My pessimistic assumptions circled my mind often and made me extremely insecure. Similar to worms and green apples, my insecurities began eating at my thoughts. To add to my deepest fear of disappointment, Jason's holiday flirting stunt glazed my mind with a sweet and sour flavor that enticed the worms to eat away with gluttony.

Breakdown

Before Jason and Lydea left for Thanksgiving, she promised me that nothing would take place. Even if nothing happened, it wouldn't have mattered, because that good ol' conscience of mine was constantly puking up negative thoughts. I used to ask myself, *How can I be secure about my relationship if I still haven't exchanged a decent kiss with her yet?* The quick pecks that we did swap were the climax of our passion thus far. I wanted to experience our first real kiss, but I resisted the temptation of my flesh wanting more. I was fully aware of the sinful man living inside of me, yearning to be awakened again.

Looking back on it, my zeal for the Lord had dropped from a nine to a six. Lydea had become my main concern and I was completely oblivious to that fact. I gave excuses for not reading my Bible when I was at home, and gradually my prayer life decreased to a few short minutes right before bed. Who was holding me spiritually accountable? It certainly wasn't my girlfriend or myself.

~ You Don't Know My Name ~

7

Insecurity appeared heavily in my heart once I remembered the foundation of lies that Lydea and I had laid. I struggled to keep my self-doubt from affecting my self-confidence. I had to remind myself that the Lord was my confidence. But like "The Ghost of Christmas Past," the devil continued to throw my old sinful ways in my face. Before Lydea came into my life, I was already dealing with unresolved clumps of insecurity from past relationships that I hadn't dealt with properly. I wanted those seasons of my life erased, or maybe they didn't need to be erased at all. Possibly, the Lord wanted me to start a new page and learn from the other pages that were already written. All I knew was, my heart wasn't created to be hurt, but to love and be loved. Why I put up with the things I did, only God knows.

I used to ask God why he allowed me to go through what I was going through, rambling on and on with questions, spilling them to the Lord. I used to ask him whatever was on my mind, until I heard a wise man say, "Ask God any question you desire, except for *why* questions. Who, what, where, when, and how are acceptable, but we, as God's creation, will never truly understand why God allows certain things to happen." In Matthew 5:45, it's written, "…he maketh his sun to rise on the evil and on the good, and sendeth rain on the just and on the unjust." So I presumed my *why* questions to God were a waste of breath. Although I was content with that verse, I continued to wonder if my troubled relationship was for purpose or punishment. For weeks, I walked with questions.

One night, while Lydea and I held a civilized conversation, one of the worst things a girlfriend could say to her boyfriend was said to me.

"Hey L, you ready for finals?" I asked, sitting on the couch at my house, chatting with her. "I know I'm not."

"I don't know," she replied. "Did I tell you what I got on my presentation?"

"Nah, but let me guess— a capital F," I answered.

"No, crazy. I got an A on it!" she corrected with delight. "The only A in the class."

"Really? That's good. Was it a final grade?"

"Yep. I have three more this upcoming week. I think they'll be easy though, Jas…"

Immediately an awkward silence became wedged in between our words. "Who?" I roared.

"Oops. I was hoping you didn't hear that."

"I know you didn't just call me him," I said infuriated.

"I'm so sorry. Both of your names start with Js and I mixed them up," she attempted to reason. "Jayden, I'm sorry. It slipped."

"I'm tired. I'll talk to you later," I quickly ended.

"You're not mad at me, are you? It slipped. Don't be mad at me, okay? Please."

"Good night, Lydea," I said in a stern voice.

"Fine," she said saddened. "Good night, Jay."

We ended the night sending bitter text messages back and forth. I couldn't believe she called me Jason. It wasn't like we had just met; we had been a couple for two full months with two prior breakups, and now she wanted to call me his name! Of all people, why him?

Days had gone by and the mishap was swept under the rug. Ironically, a refreshing song by the talented R&B singer Alicia Keys blessed the radio waves and the incident immediately pinched my thoughts. The more we heard this catchy tune, the more we liked it. Weeks later, my girlfriend messed up my name again as the song and video for "You Don't Know My Name" seemed to play everywhere I went. This great song sounded so awful at times. It replayed in my head, reminding me of my unique and painful relationship.

Breakdown

The number one unspoken rule of dating, courting, or marriage is never call your partner the wrong name. There's a feeling of worthiness that can either be built up or torn down just by acknowledging this simple and important rule. I repeat, never call someone you're dating the wrong name, especially not the name of an ex or even a disliked best friend. Don't do it! There is power and purpose found in a person's name. Don't hesitate to politely correct an individual when they've mispronounced or mislabeled you. Your name is what gives your life its legacy. It's your identity.

For instance, let's say you've been transferred to a new department at your job. You are introduced to your new department head, and the first impression goes just fine. Days later, you realize that your workload has been increased, and to add to your problems, your new boss calls you a name that is not yours. Not once, not twice, but constantly. You correct him, yet no change is made. This was how I felt, but ten times worse because Lydea was my girl. Every time she stabbed my dignity by calling me the wrong name, I eventually forgave her and acted like it had never happened.

~ Honest Surprises ~

8

The last few weeks of the semester had arrived and my classes were still kicking my butt. The rumors about my upcoming Trigonometry and Fortran computer programming finals were intimidating. Can any college student relate to preparing for a six-hour final exam? I have my hand raised. My Cost Estimating course was a must-pass and the hours spent cramming and reviewing in the library were countless. It's what the old-timers call "burning the midnight oil." Unfortunately, my poor ability to retain information was the cause for my elongated study time.

One evening, Lydea left to get food with Jason, as I sat at the table alone with her books, angry. But once she returned with a bag of food for me, my anger vanished. How could I hold a grudge if I was getting something out of it? *Free* and *food* are my two favorite words. Sadly, though, Lydea wasn't the one paying for the food I was eating. This truth came out the moment after she joined me.

"Where'd you get all those bills from?" I questioned while she counted her money at the table.

"The guy behind the register broke the fifty that Jason gave me. Look at this," she said resting her Gucci purse on the table, letting off a deep sigh. "All ones and four-fives."

"Why did Jason give you money?"

"Who knows? He's been doing it since my freshman year. Sometimes I'll even see a hundred."

"You aren't lying are you?"

"No, I'm serious. He gives me money."

"So you're telling me, *you* bought the food I'm eating, but Jason's the one who paid for it?"

"Yeah, I guess. Or it could be the other way around. It depends on how you look at it," she replied.

I shook my head, hiding the bag of food under the table and went back to reviewing my notes.

Hours later the librarian assistant tapped our table. "Excuse me," she said. "We're closing up in five minutes. The twenty-four hour study hall is open downstairs."

"Thank you," Lydea responded, stretching her arms.

"Hey, babe, you mind keeping me company down there?" I said, shutting my notebook. "I need to add some details to my problem analysis project. Say yes. Say yes."

"Jayden, you better be glad this is exam week and I still think you're cute," she said standing up, slapping the back of my neck.

"Hey!"

"It feels so late. What time is it, anyway?" she asked.

"It's a little before eleven. And I'm glad you still think I look good. If that was a compliment then I'll take it," I told her, pushing my chair in. "Thanks for staying. You know how the 'Nap Lady' likes to visit me when I'm doing schoolwork."

"Yeah, well, don't be surprised if she visits me instead," Lydea yawned.

"That's cool with me." I lifted her books from the table. "I got ten minutes worth of sleep in class today, so I'm good. We got everything?" I said, walking towards the elevator to join the other students, looking back at our table. Once we sat down in the 24-hour study hall, we spread our notes across the table and didn't leave until three that morning, determined to conquer our finals.

The following day, while Graham and I waited in class for our German Trigonometry professor to appear, Lydea was the hot topic.

"She hasn't told you yet? Aw man, it was bad," he emphasized. "No lie, bruh. Your girl was lumped up for about two weeks back then."

"Stop playing, G," I said, skeptical.

"Jay, I ain't gotta reason to lie. Lydea's last boyfriend knew that her and Jason were mad tight and he couldn't take it. He lost his temper, and well, end of story."

"Now you know I'd never hit that girl, so what does her last relationship have to do with me?" I said with composure. "I'm Jayden. No girl would disrespect me like that. I treat all my girlfriends well. She has no reason to do dirt behind my back, right? Right?"

"Call it what you want, man. Lyd is *your* girl now. Remember that," Graham concluded as our professor entered.

Great, I said under my breath. *My girl. Just great.*

Later that night, Lydea and I got away for a much needed break. Our high maintenance night on the town was dinner and a movie. A near by Caribbean spot was on the menu. As we ate from our high-backed booth, we watched a set of twin toddlers, colorfully matched, play tag around their parents near the register. Directly behind them moseyed an affectionate elderly couple, with a marathon-type love. Lydea and I snickered at their appearance, hiding the shameful truth of our dysfunctional three-way relationship with Jason.

"Hey, what time does *Gothika* start?" my girl wondered, wiping her hands with her napkin.

"Halle Berry starts at 9:10," I said, glancing at my watch, grinning. "Are you ready? Let's go."

We made the short drive to the theatre and parked right up-front, something that never happens. Soon after, standing in line to buy our tickets, a middle-aged couple approached us.

"Excuse us," the lady interrupted, wrapped in fur. "Were y'all planning to see *Gothika*?"

"Yeah. Uh huh," I replied, a little startled.

"Good. We have two extra tickets if you would like them. Our friends can't make it."

"Really?" I glanced at Lydea, and then looked back at the woman. "*Sure.* Umm, thanks."

She handed the tickets over, and we thanked them again, stepping out of line. The night was going great so far. We walked through the corridor, as onlookers followed us with their eyes. The two of us eventually sat down with our restaurant cups in hand and waited for the film to start. For the first time, we actually arrived early to a movie.

While the movie was going on, I caught a whiff of my lady's lightly scented perfume. I leaned over and whispered in her ear, "Why you smelling so good tonight, girl?"

"I always smell good," she assured, with her eyes glued to the screen. "You know that."

"Mmm hmm." Staring at her facial features, I prepared my lips and moved closer. "Can I get a kiss?"

Being as close as two theatre seats would allow, she slowly turned her head, and we locked eyes. "No. Watch the movie," she whispered in a direct manner.

Hold up. Stop the film! Did she just tell you no? My pride hollered. *She just shot you down in the theatre!*

I watched Lydea leisurely turn her head back to the screen as I did the same. *This girl just messed up the night,* I said to myself.

After the movie was over, we drove back to campus and only the radio was heard. Like any other night, I pulled into the dormitory parking lot and turned off my car so we could talk. That night was no different. However, it ended in such a way that even I couldn't have predicted.

"So did you enjoy the movie?" I asked, projecting my voice over the commercial on the radio.

"Yeah, it was really good. A little too creepy for me though. Did you like it?"

"Well, Halle was in it, so you know—"

"Did you like the movie? Not Halle!" Lydea shouted, twisting in her seat. "That's so typical of a guy to say that. Goodness."

"I liked the movie, dang. I'm joking," I expressed, lifting my hands in surrender.

"Yeah, whatever," she said with an attitude.

Minutes went by and there was a must-ask question that was bouncing in my mouth. I took a deep breath and looked at her in my passenger seat, arms folded. With candor, I asked, "Why didn't you kiss me earlier?"

"I don't know," she quickly responded.

"Lyd, I'm serious. We've been a couple since October and we haven't even really kissed yet. What's wrong with me? Do I have halitosis? Are my lips chapped? Am I ugly? What is it?" I questioned, growing irritated by her careless body language.

"Jayden, I was watching the movie."

"So was I! I can't ask for a kiss? I am your man, right?" I tested, turning the radio down.

"What kind of question is that? You know you are."

"So why don't you treat me like I am? Is it your friend? He's the reason I'm getting treated like this, huh?"

"Don't do this," she said, shaking her head. "Don't mess up a good night."

"What? You messed it up when you told me no! For two months, I haven't touched you in any kind of way to make you feel uncomfortable. Yet, the moment I ask for an effortless kiss, I can't even get that. Talk to me, Lyd. What's up with you? All my lips wanted was some attention, and all they got in return was an invisible hand in the face. Do you still want to be with me or what?"

"Yes, I still want to be with you. I've wanted to be with you from a year ago. I don't know what's wrong with me. I guess I still have my wall up a little."

"*Why?*" I said with much air.

"Well, I-I…" she stuttered, doubting her answer.

"Well, what? We've talked about this before."

"Well, Jason still tells me things. He says I shouldn't give you my heart because you might hurt me."

"Who is he to tell you that?" I objected.

"I know I shouldn't listen to him, but—" Lydea paused. "You know what, I should go," she said, cutting herself short as she gathered her things.

"No, no, no. Don't go yet." I restricted her left arm. "We're still talking. Finish what you were saying. Talk to me."

She calmly put her purse back down and leaned back in her seat, giving off a short grunt. Simultaneously, thunder began brewing as rain crackled against my windshield.

"Will you promise not to get mad?" she asked.

"Just say what you gotta say." Right then, I knew it was something I didn't want to hear.

"Don't get mad at me, okay?" she said looking into her lap. I glanced out my window and saw a group of students shuffling through the grass as I waited to hear her breaking news. "The Saturday after Thanksgiving, Jason and I drove to New Jersey and—"

"Saturday?" I interrupted.

"Let me finish!" she yelled. "We dropped off my Maxima at my father's house in New Jersey because he said I didn't deserve the car anymore. We left there and rode into Virginia, stopped to eat in Richmond, and ended up getting lost. It was already late, so Jason decided to get a room for the two of us until the morning."

"What!" I said, surprised. "That's not what—"

"I know. Just listen. Nothing happened," Lydea exclaimed, making her innocence known. "I promise. I made sure of that. It was nothing like that, okay?"

"I don't want to hear this." I looked away.

"I have to tell you. So, while we were watching TV in the room, he called me over and placed me on his lap. And then, umm," she paused to gulp. The knot in her throat was loud enough for me to hear her swallow. "He leaned over and kissed me on my cheek. Then I leaned over and…returned an innocent thank you peck on his cheek also, but he turned his face and tried to kiss me on my lips. Once he did that, I jumped up and went back to the other side of the room. I was so upset. He'd been flirting with me the whole trip. I wasn't putting up with it. Believe me, I know how he can get."

While she set her guilt free, her words grew faint to my ears. Why did I have to hear her terrible honesty?

"Are you mad at me, Jayden?" she asked, breaking the silence and reaching for my hands.

"Don't touch me," I snapped, knocking them away.

"That was it. I promise." She reached again. "I'm being honest. Nothing happened. I swear."

I sat in a trance with tightened fists, watching the rain trickle down my windshield. "I can't do this any more," I said with a raspy voice.

"Nothing happened!" she screamed. "I swear it. I didn't do anything wrong."

"I can't do it!" I yelled, striking my steering wheel. "I just can't. This hurts too much. You knew what would happen if you told me that trash."

"Why are you doing this to me again?" she bawled. Not even waiting for an answer, Lydea grabbed her purse and violently got out the car. I got out as well, trailing several steps behind her. The rain increased. She spun around and raised her voice. "Why are you following me? Go home. You make me sick."

She yelled at me as I continued to follow her, not saying a word. I must've looked so foolish. I eventually returned to my car in a state of confusion. I was finished with this relationship. I questioned the Lord the whole ride home. Who could've imagined three breakups in just two months?

Breakdown

I can see now why people don't always tell the full truth. The truth hurts, plain and simple. I hated hearing Lydea's honest surprises. I never knew what was going to come out of her mouth. Anytime she would start out with the line, "Will you promise not to get mad?" I really didn't want to hear it. Nevertheless, I needed to. I had to hear her morsels of truth. If she didn't tell me her hidden secrets, then I'd be deceiving myself, thinking my girl was someone that she wasn't.

"Be honest," I'd remind her. "Keep it real with me," I'd tell her. "You don't have to hold things back," I'd say. "Remain loyal and transparent in our relationship and you'll have no reason to cover anything up," I explained. "You'll be an open book, Lyd."

Because the darkness was brought to the light, I had to remember the power of forgiveness. There were times I gave the gift freely and other times when I selfishly held on to it. I always had possession of this gift, but I was selective in giving it away. Once I understood Jesus' view on forgiveness I realized that giving it away wasn't an option, it was mandatory. So when I forgave Lydea for her terrible honesty, Jesus, in return, forgave me when I repented to him with *my* terrible honesty. Isn't that something? Such a fair dealing judge God is!

~ Q and A ~

9

I had a decision to make and it had to be the right one. I knew the relationship that I had gotten myself into was just as easy to get out of. I was making it harder than it should've been. I blamed myself for Jason still being in the picture. I acknowledged my slender 5'10" frame didn't make me the most intimidating guy on campus, so I never inflated myself to be anything more. I had told Jason not to cross his boundary, but who was I to him?

The weekend Lydea and I were broken up, I worked at the pet store, ringing up bags of cat litter and dog toys, positive that she and Jason were together. Things had to change. When I wasn't with her, I had to deal with Jason being with her. It felt like she had another guy on the side, but I could never admit to it. It was their time together that ate me up the most. I tried to remain optimistic throughout this strenuous relationship, but my optimism wouldn't last.

All weekend long, I anticipated my regular Sunday morning church service. My heart longed for an answer to my question: to stay or not to stay? I was praying for a word from the Lord that would put me on the right track with this girl. The early service was in motion and I gave full attention to the sermon given by my pastor. When it ended, I received nothing close to what I needed to hear. I strolled out the exit doors, determined to get from God what I was in search of—answers. I needed answers. If the Lord hadn't given me a purpose, I would've left the relationship months ago.

I walked toward the church gym, where my young adult Sunday school class met. My young adult pastor gave his message with a few scriptures, still nothing grabbed my attention except for the verse from 2 Corinthians 10:4 that mentioned the term *strong hold*. Hmm, could this unnatural pulling force towards my girlfriend merely have been something that I couldn't get loose from? Or was she the one who couldn't break free from Jason's grip? I analyzed this particular verse, still I remained confused.

I considered chatting with my cute freckled, red-haired Canadian friend, Brandi, after class, but I knew her advice would be biased. She had already expressed her opinion to me, predicting that Lydea and I weren't meant to be together. So that morning I deliberately avoided her. Once class was over, I walked to my car with my head hung low, kicking the loose rocks along the pavement. Not far behind me trailed a guy from class. I turned to look and he instantly spoke.

"Hey, bro. It's Jayden, right?" he said loud enough to stop me in my tracks.

"Yeah, we met last Sunday. And you're...Marcus?" I hesitated to make sure.

"Yeah, that's right. I noticed you all slumped over, man. You look burdened. Wanna talk?"

Wow, where did you come from? my heart wondered. *Are you the answer to my prayer?*

"Man, it's so funny you ask," I told him. "I gotta situation and I was hoping to leave this morning with clarity. Maybe you can help."

Marcus and I stood in the middle of the church parking lot for what seemed like an hour, but was actually no longer than 25 minutes. Although he knew nothing about Lydea or myself, I informed this well-groomed, 30-something-year-old, military man of all the madness that was going on in my relationship. I listened carefully to his words as if he were a wise counselor. I informed him of our three breakups and how she had jacked up my name with her best friend's. I even explained how God spoke to me through a dream and how he wanted me to introduce Lydea to him, as well as show her what a true Christian could be like. I knew I was coming up short with what the Lord had asked of me; still I continued to fill Marcus in about my dilemma. He bounced right back with interest. "So, about this guy friend of hers, can you trust your girl around him?"

"Well, it's not that I can't trust her," I responded. "To be honest with you, Marcus, I can't trust him. This dude is a temptation in a way that I can't see."

The topic of temptation transitioned us onto the scripture about the strong hold. At the end of our conversation, Marcus raised one last question, which led me to my decision. He zipped up his winter coat and simply said, "So, I guess the real question to ask is, have you accomplished what God has asked of you yet?"

My tongue couldn't lie. "No," I told him, shaking my head. My mind was blank. There was nothing left for me to say. I was nowhere close to fulfilling the purpose that God had given me. Deep down inside, I still wanted Lydea to wholeheartedly meet Jesus.

Sticking my hand out to shake his, I humbly said, "Hey, Marcus, man, I really appreciate this. You don't know how much I needed this conversation. Your advice was what I was waiting to hear all morning."

"Jayden, no problem. All I did was ask the right questions. I'm glad I could help. Let me give you my number so you can contact me if you ever need to vent. I wish y'all the best, bro. It sounds like you really like her."

"Yeah, I do, man," I smirked, patting myself down, feeling for my phone. "I just don't want to feel this pain anymore. You feel me?" I sucked my teeth. "Hey, you gotta pen on you?" I asked him, still patting my pockets. "I must've left my phone in my car."

"Yeah, let me scribble my number down for you."

After we exchanged information, I returned to my car, feeling much lighter. I paused before turning the key in the ignition. I pinned my Bible to the steering wheel and stared at the cross that was engraved in gold trim on the front cover of it. "Thank you, Lord," I praised, quoting Psalms 18:6: *"In my distress, I cried out to the Lord; yes I prayed to my God for help. He heard me from his sanctuary; my cry reached his ears."* I then cranked up my Honda and headed home.

Later that evening after work, I called Lydea in her dorm and told her how my day had gone. I shared my open thoughts about our relationship, avoiding any offensive finger pointing or blame. "Hey, Lyd, I wanna apologize for Friday night," I said. "My confidence tends to be a little unstable at times, you know? I guess that's just the way I'm wired."

"I see that. Your confidence is unstable most of the time, Jayden. We gotta change that," she added, as Lauryn Hill's *Miseducation* album played in the background of her room.

"I know. I'm working on that. It's not easy, but—I wanted to let you know that my feelings are still strong for you, baby girl. They're ridiculously strong. And honestly, that's all I want in return. Can I get that from you?" I requested.

"Jay, you've always had my feelings. How about I give you my heart. Is that what you really want?"

"Yeah, gimme that too. And if I give you mine again, you gotta take good care of it, aight? It's breakable."

She rejoiced in her sweet accented voice and took me back. I was glad she was happy. Still, I had mixed emotions. I was single-minded in carrying out the Lord's commandment, but I knew my trembling heart was fearful of going through the furnace again.

Breakdown

Allow me to pass on some advice. Be careful what you ask God for because as miraculous as it sounds, he does answer prayers. During the past summer months in Atlanta, I had prayed for a lady to walk into my life and to my fortune, I received Lydea, a beautiful girl who tested my righteousness in every fashion of the word. Then I had prayed for an answer that weekend in church, and I was provided with Marcus, a messenger of the Lord, whom I have yet to see again since that day.

I do believe the last question that Marcus posed was exactly what I needed to hear. I had a purpose. Obeying God should've been my top priority. Only by God's grace was I able to create enough strength and joy within my heart to change my perspective on my relationship. Instead of complaining about the rusted jewel that was handed to me, I began double-coating my relationship with colors of optimism. It was around this time that I was given a glimpse of the painting that God was creating. I was clueless as to what he was showing me, but if I hadn't altered my perception on my relationship, many significant colors would have been left off of the mental image that God used to change my life.

~ Christmas Break ~

10

The semester was finally ending after stretching for four lengthy months. Our classes were finished. One afternoon during the last week of the semester, Lydea called me.

"Hey, babe, how are you?" she asked, while I sat at home, exam free.

"I'm cool. Here at the crib playing with my Doberman. What's going on? You chillin'?"

"Yeah, I'm fine. Nothing much. I just had a quick question. Umm, would it be all right with you if I stayed with Jason and his family over the Christmas break?"

"What?" I choked. My mouth didn't even answer her. "Call your folks, man. Don't play like that. That ain't funny," I spit back, ignoring her question while she giggled.

"I'm joking. Don't get so wound up. I'll be staying with my Uncle Carlos in Jersey. That's good news, right?"

"Woo hoo. Praise the Lord," I replied in a monotone voice. "Yes, it's good news, but that mess ain't funny."

Sadly, her transportation to Camden, New Jersey, came from Jason. The two of them were accustomed to traveling together and it was nothing out of the ordinary for Jason to be her taxi driver. He was already known amongst her family, unlike me. Actually, he was so familiar that her Uncle Carlos welcomed him to stay the night until he was ready to leave for Philadelphia the next morning. I still can't shake loose from my memory the tantrum that was recorded that night while Lydea and I spoke over the phone.

"Jason, go to sleep! You have to drive tomorrow, boy," she shouted while her friend persisted to get her time. I could hear his voice begging outside of her room, wanting her to stay in the basement with him. "I'm not going down there. Go to sleep, Jason! What is wrong with this boy?" she asked me in an aggravated tone.

A while later, I heard her bedroom door slam open and hit the wall. It was him! And if I wasn't mistaken, I heard whimpering in the background. I wish I could've been a bug on the wall to witness the two of them with my eyes. I wondered what all the craziness was about? What did he want with her?

"Can you please just talk to me?" he begged in a desperate manner.

"Jason, why are you up here?" she asked him.

"Lydea, get off the phone and talk with me," he yelled as his tantrum grew. "You've been on the damn phone all night! Please." He threw his emotions all over the room, complaints mixed with anger. He wanted my lady's time and there was nothing I could do about it.

"Jayden, this boy's getting on my nerves," she directed into the phone. "Let me go, okay?"

"Why? What does he need to talk with you about? What's wrong with that dude?"

"I'll tell you later," she whispered. "Oh my goodness. He's seriously crying over here. I'll call you tomorrow, Jay."

"Fine. Put him in check, please," I demanded.

"Okay, I will. Good night, baby."

We hung up, and believe me, going to sleep that night wasn't easy. My mind wandered in a thousand directions. Once Lydea told me that Jason had left the following morning, I felt a weight lifted from my shoulders. The vibe I received through the phone that night was indescribable. Did he even care that I was on the phone listening? It was as though he couldn't rest until she comforted him, similar to a young child reaching out to a nurturing mother.

"Lyd, what was all that about last night?" I pressed the next morning, trying to squeeze a few words out of her.

"*Nada, no te preocupes*," she said, as her usual response of *don't worry*. "Jayden, he always acts like that."

Along with the rest of the junk from previous months, I swept that event under the rug as well. My bitterness withered away the more Lydea and I spoke during the last few crawling weeks of December. Separated by several states, the telephone became our primary method of communication. We spoke morning, afternoon, evening, and night. I kept the cordless house phone glued to the palm of my hand. Conversely, Lydea's uncle made her use her cell phone due to his house phone not having call waiting.

The night before Christmas, laughter was exchanged for sorrow when she confided in me about her mother. Lydea brought up memories of her childhood with her mom during Christmas time and how they used to bake cookies and decorate the tree together. Imagining the two of them spending time as mother and daughter made me smile. I sat silently and listened to the words of this broken girl. Her story fractured my spirit. I became even more compassionate towards her life than I already was. In a bland voice, she retold the afternoon of her mother's funeral.

"My dad stole all the sympathy, Jay. My entire family ignored my presence," she shared. "No one talked to me, not even my own father. I had no one as my crutch. Do you know what it feels like to be eighteen and without an outlet?"

"Nah, I can't say that I do," I replied, realizing that she had kept her emotions bottled in for some time. I remained quiet as she opened her soul.

"That's when Jason came into my life and listened when I spoke," she added. "He became the company that I needed when I was alone my freshman year. He was there for me when my family wasn't. He gave me his shoulder when no one else would."

The way she boasted about Jason's friendship made me think that she still owed him something after all this time. Isn't that why true friends are placed in our lives—to be crutches? Why were the two of them competing in a game of give and take, as if one couldn't out-give the other? The type of friendship they had put strings on the favors they did. Whether it was transportation, finances, food, shelter, schoolwork, or quality time they offered, it always had to be returned. Tired of hearing about Jason, I flipped the topic back to her mother.

"So, babe, tell me a little more about your mom. Have you dealt with her being gone yet?" I asked with caution, understanding that this was a sensitive subject for her.

"Well, I still struggle with the fact that she's not around for me," she said. "All the simple things, like phone calls and visits; they can't happen now, you know? It's gonna be real hard to walk across that stage for graduation knowing that she's not there to take my picture."

"I can't even imagine how that feels," I said, gently. "If you don't mind me asking, how did she die?"

"My mom was in a car accident that left her extremely mangled," Lydea said, rewinding the scene of her mother being in intensive care, as she sniffled frequently. "I couldn't look at her like that. I decided that my first visit would be my last one until she recovered. But once I left her room, the nurse pulled me aside and crushed all hopes of my mom living a normal life again. Days went by and I still refused to visit her." Lydea paused to catch her emotions. "Then, my dad woke me up in the middle of the night and broke the news that she had passed away. Jayden, I swear, it felt like Novocain covered my bones. It was a feeling that I wish you never have to experience."

I listened, sitting on my bedroom floor with my back against the mattress. Eventually, our conversation lightened up and shortly after we said our good-byes for the night. While I slept, my lady strolled through my dreams. Her burdens were planted deep inside my spirit. Daily, she resided in my heart.

In no time, the end of the year had arrived, and Lydea and I were still on good terms. On New Year's Eve, at a quarter to midnight, we spoke over the phone while a friend of hers named Sean, swung by her uncle's house. Just knowing that Sean, her "dream guy" was there, made me tentative.

"Hey, Jayden, let me call you back in one second, okay?" she said, speedily rushing off the phone. "Bye."

"I'll wait—" I blurted, with the phone to my ear, hearing a clicking sound seconds later. "Oh no she didn't."

Moments went by and my cell phone rang. "Okay, I'm back," Lydea breathed. "Sean just left."

"That was quick," I responded, standing in the living room with my family, who were all holding up their glasses of champagne, waiting for the ball to drop.

"You see that? You can trust me," she said, with under a minute remaining until midnight. "It was just the two of us before my uncle came back downstairs. It was awkward, but I stood strong, Jay, and now he's gone."

"Why was it awkward?" I smoothly commented. "Was it because your dream boyfriend was on the phone?"

"Yep." She giggled. "That was it. Thirty-two seconds left until the New Year. This is so exciting."

"Hey, you told him that you were on the phone with your boyfriend, right?"

"No. Was I supposed to? He didn't ask."

Breakdown

Lydea's actions and words, or the lack thereof, made it clear to me that she hadn't been in a committed relationship before. Her *dream guy* didn't have to ask *who* she was talking to for him to know. She could've told him if she felt motivated to. I thought we had matured past that stage, but I guess I was wrong.

I presumed that Lydea's previous relationships had at least birthed the emotion of love, but she surprised me by blatantly admitting to never experiencing true love before. Falling in love was a mystery to her. I thought to myself, *Wow, this fine college girl, who could make a grown man melt, hasn't fallen in love yet?* Even I could confess and say that my past girlfriend and I had walked down the dirt road of relationshipville. Who hasn't experienced love at least once?

After this fact was revealed, I struggled to believe it. Since Lydea hadn't fallen in love before, I sought the reason for the wall stationed around her heart. Although the reason remained veiled, my search continued. I began to fall deeper for this mysterious girl who had a hold on my heart. As the saying goes, "It is better to have loved and lost, than to have never loved at all."

~ *Temptation and Opportunity* ~

11

After several weeks of being apart, I began to miss Lydea's physical presence. Weeks into January, I anticipated her return to Virginia. Her pictures in my phone weren't enough; hearing her voice wouldn't do either, yet they were all I had.

"So, Jay, when are we gonna swap our Christmas gifts?" she wondered, as we spoke via phone.

"Hmm, it depends," I answered from the break room of the pet store, sitting near two co-workers. "When are you coming back?"

"Well, Jason and I are driving back to Norfolk this Saturday. So, maybe next week sometime we can go to the mall and pick out something nice. Does that sound good?"

"Yeah. That sounds good," I agreed.

Little did she know, I had already purchased her gifts: a manageable-sized Bible, along with an all expenses paid trip to New York City with my young adult church group. I knew a Bible and a winter trip weren't typical post-Christmas gifts, but I didn't let that dissuade me. Diamonds and pearls would have to wait.

The evening Lydea and Jason returned to Virginia, she called and left me a message. "Hey, Jayden. It's me. Just letting you know that, umm, I won't be on campus tonight. I really don't feel like going through the hassle of putting my clothes away and making my bed and all that, so we were thinking about getting a room here in Norfolk until tomorrow. Call me back when you get off, okay? See ya."

What did she mean when she said, "*We* were thinking about getting a room?" I knew Jason wasn't staying there. The minute I left my job I called her back.

"Hey, babe," she answered.

"Hey, I got your message. What were you saying again about getting a room?" I blasted, catching her off guard.

"Well, Jason's tired and so am I. Plus, I really don't feel like being in my dorm tonight."

"C'mon!" I said angrily, getting into my car.

"He's paying right now. I can't tell him no."

"Yes. Yes, you *can* tell him no, Lydea! It's not that hard," I yelled. "Why are you letting him pay in the first place? Campus is less than ten minutes from any hotel in Norfolk. And let's not forget you have a boyfriend. Hello? Remember me?"

"Jay, you worry too much."

"Why do you do this? It's your first night back."

"Learn to trust me and you'll stop worrying," she barked. "Are you still coming by to see me or what?"

I moaned. "That was the original plan, right?" I said leaving the parking lot.

"Right. So, I'll see you soon. I'm at the Days Inn, near the mall. Cheer up."

"Oh, *I got your cheer*," I challenged.

"Bring it," she said, mimicking the cheerleader movie.

"I'll call you when I'm close by."

"Okay. See you soon. Cheer up," she repeated.

By 9 p.m., I arrived at the hotel and circled the parking lot, looking for her room number. I eventually parked and walked tensely up to door 262. I knocked, thinking to myself, *What am I doing here?* Seconds later, Jason swung the door open and grazed my shoulder. No words were said. No eye contact was made. There was an understood, "I'll be back," that wasn't articulated. It felt strange walking into the same room that he was leaving.

I turned to Lydea and we greeted with a warm hug.

"Hey, girl. Let me get a good look at you," I said, as she spun around with her hair pulled back in a bun. "Good to see you, babe. Too bad we're not on campus."

"It's good to see you too," she said. "Let's not go there tonight, okay? Would you mind helping me organize my CDs? My music is *so* out of order."

"Whoa," I said, glancing at one of the beds. "Are all these CDs yours? Where do I start?"

"Start with the Ms. I already started the As."

We sifted, sorted, and commented on her CD collection for a long while. The late hour mysteriously caused my thoughts to wander. I envisioned myself slowly peeling her clothes off. The old Jayden was making his way back into the room. I tried to control myself, but my flesh didn't ease up. Soon after, my mouth opened. "You mind if I take a shower?"

"Go ahead," she said from the other side of the room, unzipping her suitcase full of clothes.

"Good. I've been around so many dogs today, I'm starting to smell like one." I laughed, walking towards the bathroom area to get undressed. I leaned my head around the wall that divided us and destructively asked, "Would you mind joining me?"

After wavering, she found herself in agreement and began to get undressed as well. While the shower heated up, I tiptoed across the room in a towel and left only one lamp glowing to set a mood. Overwhelmed by the opportunity that I was clearly taking advantage of, I stepped into the steam-filled shower with Lydea.

I couldn't believe it. Just last semester, for three long months, we didn't even get close enough to touch. What am I saying? We didn't even kiss, for crying out loud. But this night put all that to rest. My flesh overpowered my spirit. Our kisses became passionate. The hot soothing water seemed to last forever. It was as if the room had our names written all over it. The span of my abstinence was approaching a full year, but I couldn't fight the feeling any longer. After we dried one another off, we slid onto the bed, and committed lust for the first time. Following our actions, we rested.

Numb to conviction and blind to sin, I was as comfortable as could be. Lydea, however, was the complete opposite. She cut on a lamp and I cut it right back off. I moved closer, and she nudged me away.

"Why you trippin? What'd I do?"

"Nothing," she hastily replied, putting her sweatpants back on. "Jason should be on his way, that's all."

"Oh, yeah, I forgot. Your *boy's* coming back. Great."

"Jayden, just get dressed, okay? It's almost one o'clock. He should be here soon."

"Why? So we can act like we're watching TV?"

"Just—"

All of a sudden, the door busted open and hit hard against the upper lock. Lydea and I jumped up. It was him! Jason must've held on to the room key. She began to fidget with the lock. "Stop pushing!" she yelled, looking back at me. The moment the lock was removed, he barged in and took ownership of the desk chair. Silence filled the room and tension promptly followed. I remained standing in front of the television, looking at Lydea, expressing my readiness to depart. I then grabbed my coat and stepped outside next to the railing, scanning the parking lot. My girl joined me, leaving the door cracked behind her.

"Call me when you get home," she said, hugging herself to stay warm, acting as if a beast wasn't in the room waiting for her.

I kissed her good-bye. "Why aren't you on campus?" I questioned with a sorrowful heart, leisurely stepping back.

"I'll be all right. Trust me."

"Call me if he tries anything. I'm serious, Lyd."

"He won't. I promise."

"He better not," I said, walking down the stairwell to my car. "He better not," I mumbled again, under my breath.

Breakdown

Truthfully, I didn't enter the relationship with the intent of getting something out of it, but that night when I did, I felt accomplished. My abstinent streak of dying to my flesh had ended and my flesh was pleased. What did I really accomplish, though? Driving home, the Holy Spirit enlightened me of two words: temptation and opportunity. These two terms are the devil's bait, which lead to many sins, particularly sexual sins. Because I've fallen victim to Satan's luring bait many times over, I've learned that when I'm tempted with no opportunity, normally nothing happens. And vice versa, when an opportunity is staring me in the face but temptation is absent, usually nothing happens as well. In this case, Lydea was my temptation and being alone in that hotel room with her became my opportunity to act on my temptation. Through the world's eyes, I achieved what most guys want from girls. Through the Lord's eyes, the only thing I accomplished was disobedience. Oh, how weak my flesh was.

Secondary to my disobedience, my blood boiled from the thought of Jason staying in the same room as my lady. He became a much bigger hurdle than I had imagined. *How am I supposed to handle this monster?* I contemplated, filled with much doubt and rage. On the other hand, Lydea wasn't out of the hot seat yet. My trust for her was extremely weak; still my feelings for her remained strong.

~ Road Trip ~

12

The semester was in action and Lydea and I were oblivious as to what to expect from it. The first Wednesday back, the two of us met in front of the Student Union after our classes.

"Well, don't you look snazzy today?" she greeted me from afar as I walked towards her with a fresh haircut, clothed in my thick new Polo jacket and blue jeans.

"I get compliments from my lady? *Wow!* Thanks, babe." I smiled as we hugged. "And look at you," I praised, pulling her away from me, giving her my elevator eyes. "Are you going to court today, girl? Why ain't you tell me?"

"Boy, shut up. This is an old outfit," she said laughing. "Hey, do you mind walking with me up to the bookstore? I need to buy my books for the semester."

"Yeah, I got you. I should buy mine too, huh?" I asked, holding the door open.

"Uhh, yeah. That would be smart. And how about when we're done, we can go to the mall and exchange gifts?"

"Consider it a deal," I told her, observing a lengthy line from the second floor stretching into the stairwell.

Long after standing in line to purchase our textbooks, we finally drove to Military Circle Mall and stepped in and out of our favorite stores. We returned to my car with bags in our hands. I popped the trunk and handed her my previously purchased spiritual gift. She unwrapped it and glared at me with a look that said, *Is this it?* But before she could say anything, I reminded her, "Hey, don't forget about our upcoming trip to New York, all right? I know a Bible isn't your typical Christmas present, but you told me that you didn't have one, so I thought this would be a good gift." I snickered, feeling a little hypocritical after what we had done the previous weekend. "It's the thought that counts, right?"

By the fourth week of January, our road trip had approached. The church bus was leaving early that Friday morning, so instead of staying on campus, I suggested Lydea stay at my house Thursday night, which would allow her to meet my family again for a second time since late October. She stayed and my folks loved her. They said we were the best-looking couple on the whole eastern shore. We laughed with them until our laughs became yawns. Then one by one, we left Lydea in the spare room for some shut-eye.

"Lyd, time to get up," I whispered Friday morning. "Lyd, get up!" I shoved her ten minutes later, finding her still under the covers. Despite running late, we made it on the bus right before our young adult pastor did the 23 person headcount. I introduced my lady to everyone, obeying the meet-and-greet rules. Moments later, our crew hit the highway and traveled along the East Coast, eager to see the Big Apple.

The prolonged bus ride to New York was miserable. The heat didn't work and several windows wouldn't close properly. An average church bus, huh? The higher up north we drove, the colder it got. Hours later, we finally crossed the Verrazano-Narrows Bridge and headed towards Staten Island in pure awe of the midtown Manhattan city lights and large mounds of snow that covered the streets. After we unpacked our bags at the reserved lodge in Staten Island, we all agreed that there was enough time to eat and scope out the historic Ground Zero in lower Manhattan before hitting the sack.

While we roamed the streets, the wind pushed us backwards. It felt awful against our faces. "Hey, this is my first time in Manhattan," Lydea said, quivering. "It's incredible."

"Really? This is my first time here without my family. And it's *our* first time together out of state," I added, with the sleeve of my thick coat arm-in-arm with hers. "Thanks for coming, babe. You're doing a good job keeping me warm."

Early the next morning, half the group split and went into the city to stand outside the NBC *Today Show*. Lydea and I, along with a handful others, slept in until 10 a.m., knowing that being well rested was the caffeine we needed for an eventful day. And eventful it was.

The ferry was our transportation across the water, and the subway was our transportation throughout Manhattan. Most of the group had never been on a subway before, so it was funny to see their expressions when a true New Yorker stood too close to them. What a funny experience that was!

Just strolling the sidewalk of New York in the middle of the afternoon stirred an energy within that was unreal. Some of us had been to Manhattan and Rockefeller Center numerous times, yet we all resembled the rest of the tourists pointing and taking pictures of the skyscrapers like it was our first time there. Once evening approached, the cold weather lowered itself and brought a hunger to our midsections. My Canadian friend, Brandi, spotted the Planet Hollywood restaurant near Times Square and effortlessly persuaded all of us to follow her.

The large portions of hot food were exactly what we needed. After paying our bills, still seated, Brandi's father asked, "You guys wanna go see the Knicks play tonight?"

"Yeah," we all agreed, thrilled at the idea of watching a professional game.

"Good. Fellas come with me. Ladies, hold tight," he commanded, adjusting the scarf around his neck. "We're gonna go check on the tickets."

Without a delay, the three other gentlemen and I stood to our feet. Brandi's father led the way as we departed towards Madison Square Garden. The second we shuffled through the entrance doors of the arena, we were informed that the first quarter had already begun and finding 11 cheap seats together was nearly impossible.

"Well, guys," our bearded leader turned around, "it looks like we should've come here before we ate. No luck with the tickets."

"Oh well," I said patting him on his back. "Just being at the Garden is good enough for me. What's next?"

"Let me call my wife," Brandi's father said. "The girls were talking about going to Macy's earlier, so let's see if we can meet them over there. Is that all right with y'all?"

The rest of us couldn't oppose. "Macy's it is," we confirmed. So away we went, battling the cold weather to meet with the ladies. Similar to the night before, the 15 degree wind chill was kicking our tails up and down the streets. Our fully covered hands and necks were hilarious. I cracked jokes under my breath about our fashion trends, but my jokes weren't funny because it was too cold to even stretch our lips to laugh. The sharp, cutting breeze was unbearable. We took dozens of pictures to capture the memories of our chapped lips and red runny noses.

After meeting the girls at Macy's, we hurried back to the ferry and returned to the lodge where the heated living room magically thawed our limbs. Sitting around the big screen TV and sipping on hot chocolate with marshmallows, we watched the Knicks contend the Miami Heat, who had acquired star rookie Dwyane Wade that same season.

By 2 a.m., everyone was in their room, sound asleep, or so I thought. The vibration of my phone on the nightstand woke me up.

"Hello?" I muttered.

"Hey…you sleeping?" Lydea asked, clear and soft.

"I was until you called. Why ain't you asleep? Look at the time."

"I know. I'm sorry. I can't fall asleep. My roommate hasn't returned yet from this morning. Have you heard from the other group?"

"Nah. I would ask my roommate, but he's too busy shaking the walls with his snoring. You should hear him. He sounds like he's gonna die."

"Come see me," she said out of the blue.

"What?"

"Come and see me. I wanna show you something."

"Are you serious right now?" I pondered the idea of leaving the men's side of the house and sneaking over to the girl's side. "That's crazy. It's late. Everyone's sleeping."

"Exactly," she agreed. "You can make it quick. I'm down the hall on the left."

I exhaled, stuck between a split decision. "Fine. I'll be down there in a minute. Bye." I hung up and sneakishly slid from under my warm covers and out the door. I tiptoed carefully down each creaking step, as my nerves danced within me, wondering what she could possibly want to show me. I walked through the dark living room, still tip toeing, refusing to make any more noise than the sound of my footsteps.

I turned down the hall and cracked open the first door on the left. "Lyd, are you in here?" I whispered. "It's me."

"Shhh, be quiet." Lydea motioned, sitting up. "I heard you coming down the stairs, boy. What took you so long?"

"I got down here as soon as I could. This is risky business." I moved towards the foot of her bed. "What did you want to show me?"

"Nothing. I just wanted to see if you'd come." She snickered.

"You are such a trip," I said reaching for her in the dark room.

"Thanks. I know. Hold up—"

"What?"

"You hear that? It's coming from outside."

"Oh snap!" I froze. "The group is back. Why you got me down here, girl?" I spun around to leave, as Lydea covered her mouth to laugh. "I knew I shouldn't have come down here."

"Wait," she whispered. "Gimme a kiss goodnight."

"What? Girl! Come here." I leaned over and exchanged a quick one with her. "We'll talk about this later," I said hastily leaving her room, sprinting down the hall, and hurdling the coffee table like a track star. Luckily, my fast strides up the loud creaking steps were nothing compared to the racket of the group coming through the front door. I dove under my cold sheets and wrapped up tight, listening to the folks downstairs complaining about the chilly weather. I chuckled to Jesus, thanking him for safely returning everyone to the lodge. I eventually fell back asleep, tossing and turning from my roommate's awful snoring.

Late Sunday morning, everyone gathered in the living room and listened to the young adult pastor give a short inspirational message. Following his words, we all joined hands to pray for a safe ride back home. The large group of us then stuffed our mouths with breakfast, packed the bus, and hit the road.

I scribbled in my notebook while on the interstate. "Did you enjoy yourself this weekend?" I asked my lady, who sat next to me.

"Of course I did. Thanks for asking me to come. I had a wonderful time," she answered sleepily.

"Good. That's good. I'm glad you had fun," I said, watching large snowflakes fill the air. "Hey, you mind staying at my place until tomorrow? I heard the weather's supposed to get worse tonight."

"Yeah, I guess. You're the driver."

"That's right. I *am* the driver," I said kissing her forehead. "So that means you'll stay with me…forever."

"If you say so," she said tenderly with her eyes closed. "You're the driver."

Breakdown

In spite of the unbearable cold weather, the frozen white streets, no Knicks tickets, and half the group leaving broke, we had a blast. Lydea loved the liveliness of New York City. Knowing me, I probably would've bowed out if she hadn't come along. I knew our getaway was a great approach to this thing called courtship. Simply being in an environment with others who enjoy life and want to do it God's way is heartwarming. There is accountability and a set standard of to-dos and not-to-dos when accompanied by a small group of quality friends. I appreciated the company that stood close by. And having my church friend, Brandi, on the trip was a good thing as well. I guess she was holding me accountable and she didn't even know it. Brandi's presence alone made it uncomfortable enough for my hands-on affection towards Lydea to be kept under control and I needed someone like that.

~ You Still Don't Know My Name ~

13

February arrived and my feelings for my lady continued to grow. One cold night, walking Lydea back to her dormitory from the Boom Box, a campus jamboree held once a week in the school's gym, I opened up.

"You know what, Lyd? I feel different," I expressed. "I don't know what it is. You might slap me for saying this, but you really feel like my girl now."

"I can't believe you just said that," she said in a surprised tone, shivering from the frigid climate. "Goodness, Jayden. How did you feel before?"

"I don't know. I mean, do you think it's from what we did a few weeks ago?" I asked with uncertainty, fitting her fingers perfectly in between mine.

"Heck if I know, but it's crazy you say that. I kinda felt like that in New York. You think it's from what we did or because we spend so much time together?"

"Maybe it's both. Who knows?" I said. "I heard about this thing called a soul-tie back in the day. Do you think we created one?"

"Soul-ties don't sound very good," she stated.

"Well, they're good for married folks. And I ain't gotta ring on that finger of yours, so you're right. It might not be such a good thing. But, I feel different. It's strange."

Driving home, I considered my bond with Lydea. Normally, I would evaluate a good relationship by the way partners treat each other, and of course, the exchange of chemistry, common interests, affection, and respect. Due to Lydea and I possessing all of these terrific attributes, the two of us constantly received praise from others about the lovely couple that we made. Our classmates would ask, "Are y'all always together?" and our answer would be an obvious, "Yeah," just to keep the accolades coming. But, no one really knew what went on behind the scenes. Our reality wasn't what people saw; it was simply what we wanted them to see. No one knew that Lydea was using Jason's cell phone because hers was disconnected from an outstanding bill over the holidays. No one knew that I had to dial his number to speak to my girl. But on the surface, we had a good relationship from what people perceived.

One morning, while lounging in class waiting for my professor, I called my girl. "*Hola. ¿Qué pasa?*" I greeted in Spanish.

"*Hola*, Jayden. Guess where I am?"

"Umm, on the toilet?"

"No, silly, the library, our favorite spot on campus. Anyways, aren't you in class right now?" she wondered.

"Yep, front row seat. My professor thinks his students will wait on him just because he's a doctor. Well, I got some news for him."

"Well, I got some news for you," she countered. "Like twenty minutes ago, an international girl from my public speaking class joined me at my table. So while we spoke, Jason's phone went off in my purse, so I answered it, and it was him calling to say hi. And I know we already talked about this, but when we hung up, he said a friendly, 'I love you.' So in a friendly way, I said, 'I love you too'."

"C'mon, Lyd. Don't mess up my day."

"No, no. I'm not trying to. This is good news. So out of nowhere, my classmate said, 'Aw, that was sweet. Who was that, your boyfriend?' And I was so startled by her comment that I just looked at her and I was like, 'No. That was a friend.' Jayden, I felt so stupid," Lydea rambled. "It took a stranger's words to finally make me feel dirty about telling Jason that I love him. I promise, after today, I won't say it again."

"Wait a minute. You're telling me it took a girl from Europe to finally open your eyes? That's ridiculous." At that moment, my Nigerian professor strolled through the door, disrupting the students' anticipation to leave. "You really gotta start taking me and you more serious. But, let me go. My teacher just walked in."

"All right. I'll see you when you get out," she ended.

"Aight. No doubt."

Around noon, Lydea and I steered our legs towards the other side of campus for some mouthwatering cheese steaks. We grabbed an open seat in the eatery and enjoyed our lunch amongst the other hungry college students.

"Girl, I could eat *three* of these," I said with my mouth full. "Mmm mm mmm."

"Slow down, Jayden. Goodness. You might choke."

"I won't choke. I'm too hungry to choke. By the way, what do you want to do this Friday for an early Valentine's Day? You wanna come back here to eat?"

"No, thank you, sir. Nice try. How about somewhere in Virginia Beach? They have nice restaurants."

"Yeah, Virginia Beach is straight," I agreed, taking another large bite. "I'll ask around for recommendations."

"Oh, guess what Jason told me? He said he was going to get me this huge box of chocolates for Valentine's," Lydea shared without thinking. "What am I supposed to do with that much chocolate?"

I stopped chewing and looked up. "Why?"

"Why, what?"

"Why do you do that? How does a simple Valentine's Day celebration get turned into a competition?"

"It's not a competition. I'm simply telling you what he told me," she said, sipping on her drink.

"You make it a competition," I said, aggravated. "Why do I have to worry about Jason giving you anything? This is a *couple's* holiday. A couple is two people. Not three."

By Friday, the night before Valentine's Day, my mind was racing. I had a decision to make. I could've either bought tickets for a gospel play at Willett Hall in the city of Portsmouth, or rented a room for the night. Unfortunately, my flesh made the decision for me, craving another minute under the covers with her. Grooming myself in front of my bathroom mirror, I faintly heard the Lord's voice in my conscience, *Is this how you show your love?* I shook with fear, trying to block the thought of the Lord knowing my motives. But who was I fooling? God knew my thoughts before I knew my thoughts. Despite him acknowledging my sinful ways, I stuck to my plans to be with Lydea the best way that the old Jayden knew how.

A pleasant dinner in Virginia Beach started the night out right. She didn't know what to expect after our meal, so when I pulled into the fancy hotel in Downtown Norfolk, her smile sparkled. Minutes later, we stood before our room door and slowly entered. The candle lit room that I prepared hours earlier looked great. We exchanged our gifts and cold toasts of grape sparkling cider. Eventually, we indulged in another night of passion. This time, there was no interruption of doors being knocked down or lights being cut on. Instead, the night ended with Lydea correcting herself in the middle of our dialogue after calling me Jason's name.

Breakdown

Have you ever wanted to punch a hole through a wooden door? Have you ever had enough rage inside of you to move a brick wall? I can honestly say that I have. It's ashame how easily a dispute can occur, even after being intimate with someone. Before the sun had a chance to interrupt the moon, I drove her back to NNU in silence. The worst part about it was, that night wasn't even Valentine's; the day approaching was. Not to mention, three other couples had already planned a Valentine's dinner with us in advance.

That following afternoon while I worked, Lydea spent her usual weekend time with Jason. Once we got together, later that evening, I hid my anger. I don't know how we enjoyed ourselves at the seafood restaurant that night, laughing with those around us, but we did. Our friends had no clue about our reality. While I regretted not attending the gospel play, Lydea yawned often at the dinner table, looking obviously tired from a lack of sleep. Being the forgiving and quick loving sucker that I was, I stuck close to her side until we left the restaurant. In the back of my mind I prayed, *Lord, tell me she hasn't been cheating on me. God, say it isn't so.*

~ Just Keep it Real ~

14

During this time, my desire to accomplish what the Lord commanded had dwindled tremendously. I was putting so much energy into Lydea, studying her character and watching her personality change like the seasons, that I was unaware of my lukewarm feelings concerning the Lord. My feelings for my girlfriend had progressively replaced my feelings for my Savior, and secretly, I was leading God on. I was walking with a passion level of 2 on a scale of 10. This was far below the standard of being Christ-like. I had become a habitually sinning Christian, who had grown cold in the Lord, and it showed through my hypocritical ways. Maurice Roberts, author of *The Thought of God*, communicates this relative experience with familiarity by saying:

> *The believer is in spiritual danger if he allows himself to go for any length of time without tasting the love of Christ...When Christ ceases to fill the heart with satisfaction, our souls will go in silent search of other lovers.* (Edinburgh: Banner of Truth Trust, 1993), pg. 57.

My soul had done exactly what Roberts had stated. I had found a false substitute for my Savior's love. On our good days, Lydea and I could talk about anything: politics, sports, entertainment, music, real estate—you name it, she knew it. But when the spiritual conversations arose they never seemed to prolong. When we spoke about God, her Catholic upbringing was interesting, but it dominated the conversation. We could always talk "church", but I didn't want to hear about her religious experiences. I wanted to hear about her relationship with Jesus, the same Jesus that I had once spent everyday with.

Despite the heart-stomping incident that had taken place the night before Valentine's, and our double facades being hidden, our spring semester was going fairly well. Our courses were demanding, nevertheless, we were passing them all. Our heavy workload kept us studious in the library, chair-to-chair, shoulder-to-shoulder.

One night, while practically sitting underneath one another, her phone rang. I immediately groaned. I knew who was calling. As expected, Jason was on his way to check his phone calls. When he arrived, he stood before our table. We watched his actions and read his eyes. We knew that he was checking more than his calls. So, of course after that day Lydea began deleting our personal text messages from the phone before he could read them again. On the rare occasions when Jason would sit with us, coated in cigarette smoke, I could feel the adrenaline rushing through my body as they conversed. My nose was buried in my textbook, while my ears remained wide-open, waiting for them to say something that I didn't need to hear.

Examining Lydea and Jason's friendship, I captured another side of her personality. It was strange how she could refrain from cursing around me because I didn't curse, yet when Jason spoke with her, I heard every type of wicked word fly out of her mouth. Jason's vulgar language didn't surprise me; I was familiar with his urban lifestyle. Yet I wondered how the same verbal spirit had attached itself to Lydea's mouth. When the two of them spoke, they became a disturbance. Many times they carried on in the library as if no one else was around. He would verbally abuse her throughout several conversations and she'd laugh as if it were normal.

"Yo, can you chill with calling my girl a B?" I directed at Jason, correcting his words.

"Jayden, he doesn't mean it," she said, standing up for her friend. "He's just joking."

"Whatever, yo. He needs to watch his mouth," I said. "He ain't gonna keep calling you out your name."

"Jayden—"

"Nah, it's cool," Jason interrupted. "Your boy's right. For once," he scorned.

Around Jason, Lydea was blind to all abuse. Hearing them bicker like children stirred my anger even more. Another night when he sat with us, I comically butted into their story with my own suggestion and she had the pure audacity to shout, "Jayden, shut the hell up!" causing random nearby students to glare at us. My eyes shot wide-open and my mouth dropped to the floor as I chuckled in humiliation.

Regardless of her sharp tongue, I still took pride in Lydea. She was the one I called my girl. When we faced each other, she gazed at the bridge of my nose, and I stared at her forehead-tickling bangs. She was the ideal height for hugs. Her athletic physique was superior to the other girls' on campus. How could I not be proud to walk with a lady like this? Her charisma had the ability to flip my feelings at any given moment. This was the relationship we had—ups and downs, sunny days and rainy ones.

Speaking of the weather, Lydea and I should've checked the forecast before attending the formal dance held on the Spirit of Norfolk Cruise at Waterside, in Downtown Norfolk. My lady purchased a stunning full-length burnt orange gown that fit wonderfully, as I coordinated in all black with a matching tie. We were by far the best looking couple on the carpet. I tried to manage my lustful thoughts, but her high-split dress continued to wink at me the whole night through.

That elegant evening stands out in my memory for two reasons. First, as dazzling as we looked, we didn't dance at all.

"I can't dance in these heels," my girl complained. "They're killing my feet."

"Okay, so take 'em off and shove 'em in your purse."

"No. I'm not dancing barefoot," she snapped. "Are you *loco*? Let's take some pictures instead. Call your friends over." I couldn't win if I tried.

The second reason I recall this night so well is because it rained for hours. The sound of the hard-hitting raindrops was heard over the thumping music. It was as if the rain symbolized our relationship. But overall, the night ended well. We left with random give-aways; still, I couldn't comprehend why Lydea told Jason that another guy had taken her on the cruise and not me.

"Hey, correct me if I'm wrong, did I hear you tell Jason at the table that someone else took you on the cruise tonight?" I asked her, driving back to campus.

"Listen, I keep certain things from him so he won't blow up on me," she admitted.

"I'm your man! You don't have to lie about me taking you somewhere. Tell him the truth. What's wrong with you?"

"I know. I'm sorry," she moped. "I should've told him the truth. I get so intimidated of what he might say."

"Why lie about it, though? Dang, Lyd. Sometimes you just gotta keep it real."

"I know. It's just hard to break bad habits."

"What bad habits?" I questioned.

"I mean, I don't like being honest with the people I'm close to because I don't want to hurt them. But see, you're different," she said. "I feel like I need to be honest with you because I *really* don't want to hurt you. I know it sounds stupid, but it's true."

"Believe me, your deception will hurt me more than your truth will. Stop living in denial," I reprimanded her. "How can you be truthful to others when you're not being honest with yourself half the time?"

"I'm trying. I really am."

"Well, you better start trying harder, girl, 'cause these lying lips of yours ain't gonna cut it."

By this time our relationship was pushing five full months, so for her to deny our close status was irrational. If Jason intimidated her, then I'm sure he didn't know about what went on in the Days Inn that night back in January or at the hotel the night before Valentine's Day. She wouldn't have dared to mention that.

Breakdown

Lydea was notorious for withholding information. She kept little secrets to herself and told false happenings just to avoid offending others. She was blind to her reality. I detected many character flaws, but who was I to judge? I was blind to my own reality. I was the hypocrite—telling the Lord one thing and doing another. I was the deceitful one. Regardless of my own hypocrisy, I urged her to press forward in truth. If I had to suffer from Lydea's honest surprises then everyone else had to as well.

Keeping it real in relationships is mandatory. It is a reflection of maturity. Maturity is a reflection of development. Development is a reflection of change. And like Apostle Paul, I used to speak, understand, and behave like a child. But once I became a man, I stopped acting like a boy. You see that—I had to change.

~ *Spring Break (Sprung and Broken)* ~

15

By mid semester, Lydea and I couldn't believe how fast our weeks had flown by. It was like time had wings. One evening, after wasting several hours on the second floor, we left the library as I held a pocket-sized calendar in my hands.

"Two, four, six, eight…Yo, we get like nine days to chill. That's crazy!" I shouted, counting the dates of our upcoming spring break.

"Yeah, yeah, yeah. You wanna hear what's crazy? I haven't eaten all day. That's crazy," Lydea griped.

"Stop playing?"

"Yes." She clutched her stomach. "Can we get a bite to eat, please? I can't take anymore ramen noodles."

"Burger King is nearby. You wanna go there?" I suggested, as we headed towards my car.

"That ain't much better, but I'll eat *anything* over noodles."

"Dang, really? Sounds serious. Don't eat me, okay?"

"Shut up, boy!" She laughed. "I won't eat you."

After receiving our food from the drive-through window, we parked and ate in my car. "Hey, guess what?" I began sharing my latest news, searching for our straws. "Word on the street is my cousin, Ricky, is gonna hook me up with another internship this summer in Atlanta! Good news, right?"

I knew by Lydea's facial expression that she wasn't too fond of this opportunity. "That's great, Jayden. Really."

"Thanks, I think so too. Internships are always a good way to get a foot in the door, you know?" I said, dunking my sizzling hot chicken tenders into the honey mustard sauce. "Hey, by the way, have you spoken with your folks about spring break? It *is* next weekend."

"Well, two nights ago, I called my dad and spoke with him about coming home for the break, but he said there was no space for me. So I called my uncle, and he said that he was going on a seven-day road trip with his fiancée."

"Hold up, Lyd. What's the real reason why your pops won't let you come home? He got space. You know that. What'd you do?"

"Jayden, I already told you. My family doesn't care. I mean, you'd think my dad and his new wife would at least provide *somewhere* for me to stay while I'm out of school," she said, chewing.

"Well, you know you can always stay with me, right? I don't think my folks would mind," I said invitingly. "Plus, it's not like you haven't stayed there before."

"Yeah, I don't know," she doubted. "Jason told me last fall that I could stay with him during spring break if I had nowhere else to go, so—"

"Oh really?" I cut her short, remembering that Jason had just moved into an apartment with a couple he knew, close to the Norfolk and Virginia

Beach border. I took a deep breath, placed my burger back in the wrapper, and slowly spoke, trying not to anger myself.

"Tell me that you didn't make this decision while we were together. I know you didn't agree to that."

"No. No. Of course not," she sprang back, putting her food down also. "We made it before. But at least I know I have somewhere to stay, right? Jay, it's no big deal."

"C'mon! It is a big deal. I ain't letting you stay with that dude for a week. My crib is wide open. You're my girl! You do know that, right?" I said testing her knowledge. "You can't choose him over me. You can't."

She knew better than to put our relationship in jeopardy, or did she? We argued back and forth for days until a decision was made.

"Okay, this is what I came up with," she said, standing outside of the Technology Building on a short brick ledge with me, filled with bliss. "Since I agreed to stay with Jason over the break a *long* time ago, it would make him really, really mad if I stayed at your place for the entire week. Sooo, what I'm gonna do is stay with you during the weekdays and stay with him for the weekend," she explained, motioning her hands like it was the best idea ever.

"Stay with me the whole time," I insisted.

"I can't. I wish I could, but I can't. I promised him."

"Lyd, it's whatever. I'm not gonna argue about this anymore. As long as we're together, I'm happy."

"That's right!" she agreed with her arms open for a hug. "If you're happy, then I'm happy too."

Days zoomed by and the weekend of spring break had approached. This was the green light, the thumbs up, and the blowing of the trumpet for a peaceful week. I anticipated our time together.

Lydea and I slept in until the late morning and planned our days with no distractions. To waste time, we ran errands and drove to different shopping centers throughout my home city. We did more window-shopping than anything else, holding hands, and wandering directionless through the different malls. Monday night was spent making wishes at the Oyster Point City Center fountain in Newport News, tossing a dollar worth of pennies into the shooting water. Our environment was incredible. I wish I had extra pages to express how wonderful her presence felt. The next afternoon, we took a trip to the Newport News City Park and dwelled in the arm length of one another. We walked trails, sat along piers, and laughed with liberty. The rays of sun found us through the abundance of trees as we took turns pushing one another on the wooden swing set.

Lydea and I talked and talked. We became verbally intimate, sharing our childhood dreams and deepest fears. We exchanged our past failures and regrets. We sat still on the swings and listened to the sound of God's creation. I dared to interrupt a moment in paradise to voice my thoughts.

"Okay, Lyd, keep it real with me. If you could tell your mom one thing, what would it be? If she stood in front of us right now, what would you say to her?"

I stared at my precious jewel sitting there with her hair glistening in the sun. Her eyes remained locked on the patches of grass that surrounded her straw, open-toed shoes. She thought long and hard, humbled herself, and said, "If I could speak with my mama again, I'd ask her to forgive me."

I twisted my face, not expecting such a heartfelt response. I listened carefully as she raised her head to speak.

"Jayden, of all the things to say, I'd ask for her forgiveness. You see, when I was sixteen, seventeen, eighteen—I used to lie about everything. I gave my mom so many headaches. It was so bad that I could actually feel my nose growing like I was Pinocchio. But I didn't care. I used to write her mean letters, telling her how awful I thought she was. But I never meant them. I didn't mean what I told her," Lydea continued, sincere as ever. "My mother didn't deserve anything I put her through; that's the thing. No matter how ugly I treated her, she never stopped loving me. I was so stupid back then. I purposely disobeyed both of my parents, all because I didn't want what they wanted for me. They'd say, 'Stay home,' or 'Don't go out with that boyfriend of yours.' But once I realized that they just wanted to protect me from this hateful world, how could I be mad?" Lydea began to weep right in front of me, breathing words of conviction. "Jay, I've done a lot of things that I'm not proud of. But above all that I've done, I regret not apologizing to my mom the most. Forgive my tears; all this still hurts."

I was speechless. I had no clue that the topic of her mother was still bubbling inside of her years later. "Her slow death gave me enough time to apologize," she added. "Everyday she spent in the hospital was another opportunity God was giving me to do it, but I never did. Every hour was a God-given hour, but I never went back after my first visit. This is the real reason why I'm on bad terms with my father. It eats at my heart every time I think about it."

That day in the park was life changing for me. I could relate. I can only imagine the number of individuals who have walked in her shoes, living everyday in regret from their youth. Prideful and selfish decisions will always lead to regrets. But, thank the Lord, humility eventually settles within us all over time.

"Lyd," I said sadly, rising from the swing and stepping closer to her. "Your mom's listening to us right now. She heard every word. She forgives you. Now, all you gotta do is ask God to forgive you," I said, reaching for her hands to pull her up from the swing. "Did you know that?" She shrugged. "But, it doesn't stop there. God will forgive you. He already has. Now, you just gotta forgive yourself."

"What do you mean?" Lydea wondered, wiping her tears. "Why do I have to forgive myself?"

"Because it's necessary. I'll put it like this: a wise man once said that choosing to not forgive someone is like drinking poison and waiting for the other person to die. So in the same words, if you don't forgive yourself, then it's like you're still drinking the poison," I told her, leaving the swings.

"Are you saying that I'm killing myself by not saying, 'Lydea, I forgive you'?" she asked with sarcasm.

"Well, sort of. I mean, as simple as this might sound, babe, Jesus doesn't want you living in self-pity everyday. Bitterness, guilt, and all that junk that's inside of that heart of yours needs to be handed over to the one who went to the cross for it. And I'm not trying to get all scriptural and stuff on you right now, but you need to know these things," I explained with understanding, as a large group of high school cross country runners jogged past us. "When you truly forgive someone," I continued, "you feel pure relief deep inside of your soul. You'll feel God actually removing the weight. That's something that we, as humans, can't do. Remember this: God is all about exchange. When we give him our sins, sicknesses, and problems, he returns a piece of himself back to us. Now that's love, huh? Ain't no better love than that. C'mon now."

"Yeah, that makes sense," she agreed. "I guess Jesus didn't go to the cross for me to be weighed down by my past or my present. You know what, though? This just crossed my mind. I think my mom must've forgiven me every time I did her wrong and I wasn't even aware of it. That's probably why it was so easy for her to love me. Regardless of how ugly I treated her, she still loved me." Lydea grinned with relief.

"I feel you. I wish all parents could forgive their children that easily. The same goes for children forgiving their parents. I used to hold long grudges with my folks, for months."

"Believe me," Lydea said, walking next to me in the direction of the orange setting sun, "I've been there, and done that."

That particular day in the park, the sky was the color of love, and the clouds were shaped like hearts. Our friendship and knowledge of one another increased volumes. Tranquility was in the air and we both smelled its fragrance. If nothing else, I was pleased. I smiled from the inside out. The moment night fell, I knew our day in the park was destined to happen just as it had.

By evening, Lydea and I were in the spare room of my house, sitting on her bed, relaxing as our free time allowed. I surprised her with my two hidden shoeboxes that were jam-packed with private letters from my middle and high school years. We took turns opening the letters from various females, anticipating what each one said. Some were simple and others juicy. I skimmed through the old love notes from past flames and handed them her way. She read them aloud.

"Dang, boy, you must've been the man back in the day!" she praised, stretched across the full-sized bed. "Are *all* these letters from girls who used to sweat you?"

I nodded. "What can I say? If you don't know, you better ask somebody, gurrrl." My smile became an outburst as I leaned on Lydea's backside, playfully pushing her closer to the edge of the bed. With quickness, she grabbed onto my upper arm, not wanting to hit the carpeted bedroom floor. I snatched her by her waist and looked into her eyes, still laughing. Without me saying a word, she heard me say, *I won't let you fall.*

After calming down, we continued to breeze through my collection of letters. "I can't believe that you kept all these," she said. "Throw some away. Ugh."

"Hey, I like to hold on to things, okay? Don't be hatin' on a brotha," I joked back, hauling another large stack of creatively folded paper her way.

"I don't want to read anymore. This is messing with my mind." She shoved the pile back towards me and stood up to wrap her hair. "I'm tired. It's almost two, Jay. Go to sleep."

"What's wrong?" I teased, stacking the letters back into the shoeboxes and rising from the bed also. "You can't hang with the grown folks?"

"Whatever. Good night, boy. I hope you like pancakes and eggs," she voiced, as I reached for the doorknob to go to my room.

"With bacon on the side." I smiled, closing the door.

The following morning, Lydea cooked an incredible breakfast. By the end of the day, my lady was ready to leave.

"Jayden, don't be offended when I tell you this," she said standing on my front porch with me, watching cars scarcely drive by.

"Tell me what? What's going on?"

"I don't feel comfortable staying at your house."

"What?" I said confused. "What are you talking about? Is my crib uncomfortable? Is it the bed?"

"Your family is too perfect," she said, looking away. "Plus, I'm starting to miss my mom again. I'm sorry, but I can't stay here."

"Hold on. For one, no family is perfect," I said stepping towards her. "And missing your mom the way you do is a mental battle that you haven't coped with yet. This is the best place for you to be. Where's all this coming from, Lyd? What about your promise? Don't stay with Jason."

"I'm breaking my promise." She gently pushed by me. "You don't know what it's like to *not* have a mother," she said. "All I have is pictures and memories, okay? *Everyday* is difficult. So, without making this a big scene, I'd like to leave. Now."

"Lydea—"

"Now! Please."

Breakdown

How can a relationship grow in trust when loyalty is absent? Can respect survive if there is no trace of loyalty? Should I be loyal to someone that I don't trust? I can't count the times Lydea put Jason before me. I had blind faith that she was being faithful. My level of trust was never 100 percent. I mean, look at our situation; how could it ever be? Our relationship was definitely lacking loyalty and the weekend of spring break opened my eyes and proved it once again.

To me, faithfulness and loyalty walk side-by-side. Being faithful has a physical responsibility attached to it. When I'm practicing faithfulness, I hold only my lady's hand, I kiss only my lady's lips, I rub only my lady's feet, etc. When I'm committed through my loyalty, it becomes more of an invisible responsibility. In committed relationships, it is imperative to breathe both loyalty and faithfulness. When my girl wasn't around, I made sure that I didn't make side phone calls to other females. I avoided being isolated with another female friend for an excessive amount of time. If I were to walk into the house of a luring woman and stay for an hour without touching her, that would show my faithfulness, but being enticed into the woman's home would unveil my lack of loyalty. When true loyalty is practiced, ultimately faithfulness is being accomplished also.

~ The L Word ~

16

After spring break, I tried to erase the resentment that I had towards Jason. I greatly despised him for being so close to my girl. To add to my daily torment, Lydea *wanted* to spend time with him. That alone kept me insecure. But there was one thing that gave me a fake sense of security. Whether it was a good or a bad week, the best way the two of us knew how to make up to one another was on Friday nights when our schedules were completed.

Dorm visitation ended at eleven, so my time was arranged accordingly. We spent the first few evening hours watching TV programs and music videos in her room, and afterwards we'd usually go pick up some food and bring it back to her dorm. Following our meals and TV shows, we turned the lights off and you know what came next. I tried to avoid the flirting and touching, but a willing kiss was all that it took. Many Friday nights ended in the same sinful manner. Lydea would then walk me downstairs to the lobby and we would exchange our good-byes.

Where was my fear of God? My conviction was almost non-existent. I used to wonder how an activity like sex outside of marriage could have such a grip on my flesh. Did I enjoy pleasing my flesh more than pleasing the Lord?

100

At that time, I didn't know. I used to silence God's voice before diving nose first into indulgence. What a sinner I was, living in disobedience.

Being sexually active had taken my mind off of whatever the problems in my life may have been. All my worries were erased once our shirts willingly came off. Sex was like medicine to ease the pain. It became extremely addictive once I allowed opportunity and temptation to whisper in my ears. My flesh ignored God's watching eyes. The lust burning inside of me was my fire. All the things I thought sex could erase or fulfill ultimately left me feeling the same on the inside; still having insecurity prick at me days later. I knew my weaknesses and my weaknesses knew me. My physical life began to conquer my spiritual life. I continued to fall for this girl who had broken my heart several times over.

One rare occasion in April, I was prepared to leave the library and pick up my parents from the Newport News Airport, when I noticed the words "I Love U" carved into the top left edge of the wooden table. While gathering my items next to Lydea, I quickly grabbed a few worksheets and piled them in a stack over the corner where the phrase was written. I hugged Lydea good-bye and went on my way. After driving through the Hampton Roads Bridge Tunnel, I courageously phoned her. "Hey, Lyd, stop what you're doing. I want you to read something."

"How?" she replied. "Aren't you driving?"

"Yeah, but that doesn't matter. Right where you're sitting, look to the far left side of the table. Lift up those sheets of paper and tell me what you see."

"Jay, I'm studying. What am I looking for?"

"Are you looking at the corner?" I anticipated.

"Yeah," Lydea said.

"Those words you see, that's how I feel about you," I said with assurance.

"What!" she shouted into the phone. "Do you really mean what you wrote?"

"No doubt," I told her, as if I wrote them. "Those words are real, girl."

After I broke the ice that day, Lydea tried to pull the L word out of me every chance she got. Call me a dancer, but I wittingly danced around the topic for a week. It was difficult to actually have those words leave my mouth. And once they did, she wanted me to say them again and again. When we got off the phone, it was expected. When I left her dorm, it was expected. Saying, "I love you," was one of those big stepping-stones in our relationship. Regardless of who said it first, the moment it was verbalized, it became another habit that was hard to break.

"Jayden, I've loved you from the beginning," she debated over the phone, claiming her feelings were stronger than mine. "I didn't say it back then because I knew you didn't feel the same. I wasn't gonna put myself out there like that."

"You loved me back then? *Please*," I said, sitting on my couch, watching ESPN highlights. "As for me, the feelings I got for you are real. They're different than what you feel for me. Your love needs to hurry up and catch up to mine. And you can stamp that, sista!"

"Whatever, Jay. You still have a wall around that heart of yours. All your insecurities are like little soldiers with rifles. How am I supposed to get past them?"

"Little soldiers? Yeah right," I denied, knowing that she was on point. My crippled heart still showed signs of doubt and insecurity. Was my mind in love with Lydea and not my heart? I honestly didn't know. I went through all the motions of being in love, with the things I did and the words I said, but was I truly in love? We held hands, gave sweet kisses when we said goodnight, and even our intimate time together seemed to be more enjoyable, but was this love that I was experiencing?

My lady and I constantly brought up this topic, going back and forth to see who would say it last before hanging up. "I love you more." "No, I love you more." "You hang up." "No, you hang up," was how we often ended our youthful phone conversations. Even around Jason, Lydea boasted her love for me. He observed his "best friend" falling in love with a young man other than himself. It was obvious, the stronger her feelings got for me, the weaker it made him.

I've always wondered how an individual could properly love someone else, being distant from the Creator of love. God holds the copyright to love. He knows the true definition of the word. I'm still confused, is love a noun or a verb? I'm still learning to love myself. How could I have truly loved her?

It was my ignorance about this whole love thing that sparked a passion within to search for the proper meaning again. My first definition of the word *love* came from others who claimed to know, such as my parents, friends, and family members. The definition came from society, and to this day, it's still very difficult to remove these worldly views of love from my mind. I was searching for love in all the wrong places. I knew that God was love and he was the giver of it, pure and unspotted. I knew that 1 Corinthians 13 gives the outline of love. I knew that pure love couldn't be found where it didn't exist. I knew the giver of it must communicate it in all aspects in which it is given, but looking back now, I wish I had held on to my fleshly showcase of love, because all it did was corrupt my display of godly love to her.

My corrupted connection with Lydea had taken me far away from where God wanted me to be. It was apparent that my relationship, my schoolwork, and my job became the priorities in my life. The swapping of the Lord for my girlfriend was unintentional. Only if I had recognized back then just how strong God's love was for me, I would have never removed him from being first.

Breakdown

How can you tell if the love your partner has for you is real? How can your partner know that the love *you* show them is authentic? Falling in love is a beautiful emotion to feel, but pretending to fall in love can be one of the most deceptive experiences that the human heart can endure. Back then, I was still searching for the definition of love in a secular way, and my words were often said in vain. Honestly, I didn't know what true love was when I was 21 years old. I merely thought I did. A majority of individuals who are double that age still do not know what true love is.

In retrospect, I believe all those feelings I felt could not have been the bona fide thing. I had an artificial love. It was tainted and unpure. We overdosed on sin, playing with the devil. We abused the purity of love by practicing the world's definition of it better known as fornication.

Retain this: while you paint the picture of a serious relationship, before you vocally project how much you love your significant other, remind yourself that once you say it, there's no rewinding your words. Once it's put on the table, it needs to be a sure thing. If I would've simply admitted that I was double-minded towards loving Lydea, then I could've avoided so much disorder. Instead, I struggled to live up to the words I expressed.

~ *April Showers Bring May Showers* ~

17

During the month of April, my rainy days were more than plentiful. Next to my worldly relationship, my classes remained a top concern. Final exams were approaching in a few short weeks, and no matter how focused I strived to be, distractions were ample.

One day, Lydea's troubled friend, Jason, swung through the library to check his daily messages and walked in on the two of us strongly flirting at our table. We saw him and quickly broke free and sat up straight. Jason's presence alone could divide our union. I don't know why I gave him that respect. On that particular instance, he sat with us and revealed a side of himself that I had always knew existed.

"Jason, are you all right?" Lydea asked, concerned, as he slothfully took his seat. "What's wrong with you, boy?"

"Nothing," he coldly responded, reeking of marijuana. His facial expression was that of a severely depressed individual. "Why do you care? It's not like you wanna help."

"I care because you're my friend," she told him. "What's that smell? Are you high again? I thought you quit."

"I did. And I'll quit again after tonight. You know what?" He knocked my pen off the table. "Forget this, yo," he said, banging his tattooed fists onto the wooden surface. "I'm done."

"What does that mean?" she worried, as I quietly skimmed the pages of my notebook, listening. "Speak so I can understand, Jas. What do you mean you're done?"

"My life, Lydea! It sucks. I dropped all my classes last week and now my job is cuttin' back my hours."

"No! You dropped school? Why?" she questioned. "We have less than a month left, Jason. What's wrong with you? You told me that you were doing okay."

"Forget school, man!" he fired back. "College is stupid. That was my second time repeating those same damn classes and I still haven't learned a thing."

"Jas, you know I could've helped you," she told him, as others sitting around us griped about their volume. I continued to sit there with my head down, acting as if I was invisible. Moments went by before Jason broke the stillness.

"Yo." He looked up and paused. "You think anyone would miss me if I disappeared?" he said in a miserable tone. "I ain't talkin' about disappearing from Norfolk to Philly, but not being here anymore, you know?"

Did I hear him right? Was he actually thinking about doing something suicidal? I flipped the pages of my notes, lending an ear to his sorrowful words. Lydea instantly leaned forward, sitting on the edge of her seat.

"What the hell are you talking about, boy? Don't talk that crazy mess! You're starting to scare me," she yelled, fearful of what Jason might do to himself.

"Nah, see, I already thought about it. I wouldn't take my life. I'd just be at the right place, at the right time, for someone else to."

I shook my head with compassion. It was apparent that Jason had lost all hope. Lydea was his happiness, but she was taken. She was my happiness and this was the venom that flowed through his veins. 24 hours later, he became the topic again. While Lydea and I studied at the same table, he walked up and slipped a note into her hand. The minute he walked away and turned down the staircase, she opened the letter. The two of us huddled over the folded paper and read it line-for-line under the table. Together, our eyes saw his neatly typed, troubled thoughts. He complained about his life and his friendship with her seeming so distant. By the end of the letter he repented to Lydea for his suicidal thoughts. Gradually, the topic of Jason's mental state died down and I went back to focusing on my classes the best way I could.

My 15 credit hours worth of classes accomplished exactly what they were created to do; stress me out. My senior project was my main concern and it was worth a huge percentage of my grade. Our class assignment was to design and assemble a life-like model of a commercial building and communicate its cost and structural information. Many hours were exhausted in making my project a success. The time I spent engulfed by my work eventually separated me from Lydea, but there was a solution for that.

"Hey, babe," I called. "You wanna come to the lab?"

"Jay, I'm in the library."

"I know, but come over *here* and study. It's me, Graham, and some other classmates. *C'mon,* it looks like they'll be leaving soon anyways. Keep me company. *Pleeease."*

"Okay, okay. Fine, you win," she said silencing my begging. "I'm on my way."

"Thanks, babe. Love you."

Shortly after Graham and the other classmates departed, Lydea joined me. My lady and I caught eyes. Our echoing voices gave us the assumption that the entire third floor of the Tech Building was desolate. After much flirting, temptation crept its way into the classroom and reached a level so high that it couldn't be ignored. The thought of doing something so spontaneous brought chills to our spines. We had the type of attraction towards one another that even five seconds alone in a closed elevator was too long. No lie, if it wasn't for the sound of a nearby janitor mopping the hallway, the two of us would've done something that we had no business doing. Somehow we controlled our hands and darted out of the classroom, snickering past the lady janitor. We raced down the stairs to release our laughter outside the exit doors. I wish every night was that memorable. That was one of very few.

Another night when she assisted me with my model, Jason appeared by himself. "Lyd, you ready?" he asked, standing at the doorway as Graham gave him a nod. "What's good, G?" he said.

"Yeah," Lydea answered. "Jayden, I'll be right back. We're going to McDonald's."

Graham and I watched her disrespectfully walk out the door with her friend. "Jay, man," Graham stood up, slamming his scissors onto the table, "how do you deal with that girl?"

"Whatchu want me to say? By the time she finished her sentence, she was in the middle of the hallway."

"I'm concerned about y'all, dog. I try to stay outta your business. You know that. But man, what was that about?"

"I don't know, bruh. You know how she can be. You've known the girl longer than I have. How do *you* deal with her?" I questioned him right back, slamming my bottle of wood glue onto the table and standing up also.

"Listen, I know her as a distant friend. You know her a lot better than I do, playboy." He gave a cheap smirk and turned away. "How do you put up with her ways, son? If I was you, I would've gone to the crazy house a long time ago."

"Yeah. I got gray hair popping up all over, man."

"I *see why*. And what's up with Jason comin' up here, snatchin' her up like that? He didn't even acknowledge you. That wouldn't be me. No, sir. I'd have that girl in check."

"Hold up, fat boy! You ain't even *gotta* girl, so you can't have anybody in check. And honestly, I don't know how I put up with Lydea. Her and her boy need to squash all this comin' and goin' trash. What kinda friendship they got?" I bounced my thoughts off of Graham, hoping that he could inform me of some dirt.

"There are some things that you don't wanna know about those two. They have a history, a past together, dog. Their friendship is too tight to break up. Although, I will give you props," he said, chuckling, leaning against the doorframe. "You did a great job coming in between 'em. I will give you that. But if Jason hasn't gone anywhere by now, he probably ain't leavin'."

"What do you mean, there's *some things* I don't wanna know about? Why didn't you tell me last year before I asked the girl out?" I exclaimed. "That's messed up, G. If you knew they were that tight, you should've told me to stay away from her. Bruh, I've put myself through a whole lot. And I mean *a whole lot*. So, if you're standing here telling me that I've wasted the last six months, then me and you are 'bouta fight," I said, half-joking with my fists up.

The longer we chatted, the more opinionated Graham became. In the middle of our discussion, the sound of Lydea's heels hitting the hallway tiles broke our dialogue. She stepped into the classroom, cradling a bag of food.

"Hey, I'm back. That was quick, right?" she said, stretching out her arm to give me the rolled-up paper bag. "Here. You owe me for those burgers. I got it with the little money that I had left," she said in a provoked tone, as if I had asked for them.

"Yeah, thanks for thinking about your man," I sarcastically responded, digging through the crinkled bag. "I'll pay you back with my love, aight?"

"What? I don't want your damn love!"

In one quick motion of words, she slit my heart in half. I stopped breathing. My insides became numb. My ears internally bled from her blow. I glanced over at Graham, making dead eye contact with him. I dropped my head and released a fake laugh, playing it off as if nothing had been said. I quickly changed the topic, internally filled with rage.

Lydea's conviction forced her to speak up once we left the building an hour later. "You know I didn't mean what I said up there, right? It slipped," she said, trailing a few steps behind me. "Jayden, I didn't mean it. I was mad at Jason and I took it out on you. I'm sorry. It came out wrong. Can you slow down and walk with me, please? I'm sorry."

Lydea's requests for forgiveness were heard so often that I could predict her choice of words before they even left her mouth. That night, I walked ahead of her straight to my car, mute.

Breakdown

Has your heart ever been ripped from your chest, creating dryness in your throat, making it hard to swallow? The feeling is terrible. Lydea's razor sharp words cut me so deep. I wouldn't want anyone to experience such a crushing feeling. Right after Graham and I had spoken about her unpredictable ways, she proved us right. Graham sat there silent, anticipating my anger to grow out of control, but it didn't. I remained quick to think, slow to speak, and slow to anger, just as scripture commands. Still, how was my mind able to think at all? My hot-tempered ego yelled inside of me. It wanted to be liberated, but I didn't release it. I simply lifted my burden to the Lord and my motive returned to my God-given purpose, which was driving me insane. I knew that my emotional obedience was a significant part of fulfilling his purpose.

~ All Questions and No Answers ~

18

How many times can a person say that they're sorry before it loses its meaning? I had heard, "Jayden, I'm sorry," from the start of the fall semester. I was beginning to lose count of Lydea's apologies. What's worse—saying something hurtful to your loved one or doing something hurtful to them? I'm still clueless.

There was one episode that took place in the computer lab of the library when I was taking advantage of a large bulk of extra credit. Once again, my girlfriend, the 4.0 honor student, pulled one of her stunts.

"Jayden, can you please hurry up?" she complained with no patience, standing over me in the crowded lab with an attitude. "Why haven't you finished those questions yet? You've been at this stupid computer for hours."

"Chill, girl. I'm almost done. All I gotta do is e-mail these answers to my professor. Gimme a minute, aight? My professor doesn't play with time. Ten o'clock means ten o'clock," I reasoned with her.

"Well, I'm giving you five minutes and I mean that. Five minutes. If you weren't so busy playin' around with your boys for the last hour and a half, you would've been done by now." My classmates, sitting behind me, mimicked her. "Are you listening to me?"

"Yeah. I heard you, girl. Dang. Aight. Five minutes."

"Good. Plus Jason is on his way, so try to hurry."

"Are you serious? Can y'all go one day?"

"At least somebody wants to see me. Can you finish what you're doing, please? I'll be waiting by the stairs." She turned and swiftly stepped out the door as I returned my eyes to the computer screen, letting off a sigh of frustration.

When I finally e-mailed the answers to my professor, I was shocked to see how much time had gone by. One moment I saw Lydea by the stairs through the glass window, and the next moment she was gone. I rapidly packed my bags and dapped up all my boys. I darted out the lab doors. I glanced left and looked right, hoping to see her waiting for me. *Where could she have gone?* I thought, jogging down the stairs. I dialed her number, trusting that she was close by.

"Hello," she said, answering Jason's phone.

"Yo, where you at?"

"I'm, umm, I'm with my friend," she uttered, while the radio played clearly in the background.

"Who? Jason? I thought you were waiting for me to finish my work! Why you gotta—"

"I told you I *wasn't* gonna wait," she interrupted. "I gave you five minutes, Jayden. And then I waited another five minutes. You never moved."

"So that gives you the right to rollout with your boy?" I shouted in the phone, holding it away from my face, pacing the pavement in front of the library. "Why do you do this? Our day was goin' good and now you wanna pull this trash. Where are you at now?"

"We're driving to his apartment. He said he had to get something. I'll be back soon. Don't leave yet, okay?" she insisted, as I stomped to my car, ready to go home.

"If you wanted me to stay, you shouldn't have left." I looked around, hoping no one saw me in such a tantrum.

"He wanted me to ride with him. I'm sorry."

Yep, there goes that word again. Sorry must've been tossed around more times than the L word. It's natural for people to apologize when they've made a mistake or a misjudgment that they acknowledge as being wrong and don't plan to repeat again. However, dealing with repetitive mistakes was what I grew accustomed to. How many times should an offense be repeated before it's no longer considered a mistake? I think two, maybe three times at the max, right? What's the approach when an individual slips up so many times that it seems deliberate?

Do you want to know how I handled it? I'll tell you how I handled it. I tolerated it. I refused to be offended by her actions. I never once accepted the hurtful things Lydea did or said to me. The little riflemen around my heart held their positions well. I knew what long suffering felt like. The mercy I gave was my strongest attribute to relating to God, and by no means was it easy to give.

My heart never received any of her practiced excuses when she messed up my name, neither. Sometimes she caught herself halfway and other times she would clearly, without a doubt, call me Jason. One week, she broke her previous record by messing up my name five times! Should this kind of mistake lead to a breakup? Should it result in personal items being thrown? Should I have allowed my anger to spark my temper? Should my temper ever take control of my actions? What should I have done? Ask yourself, how do you handle verbal abuse from an individual whom you *claim* to love, and who *claims* to love you in return?

"Jayden, c'mon. I mess up Jason's name with yours too," Lydea justified.

"Whatever, girl. Mess my name up one more time and I'm gone," I told her, pointing my finger in her face. "I ain't playing." Yet, when that once more became a once more, I'd just get upset and stare at her, irate.

She spoke without thinking time and again. It was hard to believe that this well-spoken honor student could have such an unruly tongue. What kind of cold-hearted girl was I claiming to love? Why did I have to hear Jason's name brought up so often? Why was I being compared to him? Why did she mix up my name with his? Why did she do things that she would later regret? Why did Jason give her his phone? Why did I stick around so long? Why couldn't he have left from the start? Why did I ever tell her that I loved her? Why wasn't I happy? Why did I bombard myself with questions everyday?

The reason I filled my brain with so many questions was because there were no answers. My spirit was weighed down. I lifted all my issues up to God, wondering why I was in such a horrible situation. I challenged my ears to listen to God's voice, praying in complete silence, but still no responses were heard. I asked Lydea the same questions I asked myself and she couldn't answer me either.

On the first hot day of spring, the both of us skipped our 2 p.m. class together and walked towards the Registration Building, better known on the yard as the "Frustration Building." We held hands as we spoke about our relationship.

"Lyd, I don't ask for much, do I?" I wondered.

"I don't know," she replied. "I guess not."

"My wish from the beginning of our relationship hasn't changed. All I've asked for was your honesty, your loyalty, and your time. That's it," I shared with simplicity. "It's not that hard. But do you realize how you carry yourself when you're not around me measures your loyalty?"

"Umm, no," she said, confused, sidestepping a large wad of gum stuck on the pathway.

"I need you to tell me the truth before questions arrive, babe. Yes, I want your loyalty. Yes, I want your time," I added. "How can I doubt your faithfulness if you're beside me every hour?"

"Okay, that right there, that's just creepy. There's no way that can happen," she gestured. "But, I mean, I understand what you're saying."

"So if you understand, then why do I only see one of my three requests? Our time is enough to keep me from complaining, but—"

"Okay. So then stop complaining," she firmly said.

"You still don't get it, do you?"

I couldn't stop complaining. I felt like we were cartoon characters with thick, dark clouds hovering over us. Was this a God thing? Could God have been keeping this cloud over our heads for direction like he did with the Children of Israel, guiding them out of the land of Egypt into the Promised Land? Whatever the Lord was up to, I had to trust him.

Mentally, I continued to observe God painting his picture. This painting had been started months earlier, but it was far from being finished. I still had no clue what the finalized product was to look like. Despite my understanding, God painted away, one stroke at a time.

Breakdown

No matter how deep I stood in the mud, I continued to call on the Lord. I understood why Jesus would pick and choose the prayers that he answered. How could I be mad at God? I was practicing fornication and still pretending to be holy in front of others. My hypocritical religious ways dimmed the light that once shined so bright. It took away the flavor in the salt that Jesus wanted me to be. I was just as guilty as the other heathens that spend their Saturday nights in nightclubs, getting hazed and intoxicated, just to stumble into Sunday's service to doze off halfway through the sermon. For so many years, I was that guy. Back then, my fear of the Lord was absent, but today I can sincerely say that those days are far behind me.

Even though my passion for God was lukewarm, he continued to reveal certain things to me about my character. My relationship with Lydea was a struggle to maintain, but I eventually realized that my obedience before the Lord was being tested. Throughout each test, I stomped through the puddles and pressed forward. As the days, weeks, and months went by, our inconsistent weather report went from good to bad to worse.

~ Sunshine ~

19

After all that had taken place during that rainy month of April, the sun was still able to shine. In order for Lydea and I to keep our passion alive, we spent nights recharging the electricity that tended to flicker.

I reminisce on the highly anticipated Alpha Phi Alpha cabaret, which had our campus buzzing. It was the biggest event of the spring semester. Anyone who was anyone at NNU was going to be there. Tickets were selling fast.

The afternoon of the cabaret, Graham and I left the Technology Building, brainstorming about how we could impress our ladies.

"What about flowers?" I suggested.

"That's it!" Graham said, animated. "I got it. How about some nice flowers? There's a great spot right down the street. You got time?"

"Yeah." I laughed. "I'm free. You trying to go *now?*"

"*Yeah.* I got back-to-back classes in about forty minutes. Now is good for me."

We stood at the checkout counter of the floral shop and listened to the wrinkled, big nosed man behind the register breakdown the meaning of each colored rose. Following our purchase of the more lighthearted pink ones, we walked back to my car, tossing creative ideas to one another on the most unique way to present the flowers to our sweethearts. So Graham, being the more amusing one, came up with an outrageous but feasible approach.

"Son, that's bananas! But I like it. Wait." I paused, standing by my trunk. "I got an idea. You know Cassell from the football squad, right?"

"Of course. Who doesn't know him?"

"Good. He's rollin' with us tonight. You wanna get him involved?"

"Yeah. That's what's up. Call him. See if he's down."

Without delaying, I dialed Cassell's number and explained the setup for the night. All I heard on the other line was hard laughter. "I know y'all boys ain't serious," he barely uttered. "It's whatever, dog. I can't wait to see this."

Hours later, the evening was finally set and our moment of glory was soon approaching. I posted by my car, clothed in my crowd-pleasing, short-collared, radiant, sand-colored suit, spotting Graham in the distance. "Yo, G!" I yelled across the parking lot, watching my round partner in crime smoothly bop across the street with his wine-red button-down shirt and sharply pressed black dress pants. His matching checkered tie and feathered pimp hat went well for the occasion. "Is Jackie ready?" I asked.

"I hope so," he hollered back, "'cause I know I am."

"I see that, Pimp Juice. Don't hurt yourself walkin' like that either. Call your girl and tell her that we're leaving soon. I'm 'bouta see where Cassell's at."

Leaning on my Honda, I dialed Cassell's number. The second he picked up, I recognized his artic blue headlights turning the corner, coming my way.

"Yo, yo! What it is? What it ain't?" he greeted.

"Hey, yo man, your whip got some nice contacts. They look just like mine. Ain't that somethin'?"

"Yeah, whatever, hater. You know I had my Accord and these contacts *waaay* before you got yours. I should change your name to Number Two, homeboy." Cassell chuckled, denying the fact that my Accord always looked a little better than his.

"I got your number two," I shot back. "Hurry up and park. Me and my boy G are straight ahead on your left. We'll see who's number two once you check out my fly suit."

"Aight, no doubt. I see you already, over there lookin' like a skinny light bulb. Get your weight up!"

"Shut up." I laughed.

Once Cassell parked, he stepped out of his mean, green Honda wearing his show-stopping patent leather gators and his gray, tailored, pinstriped suit. He carefully patted down his fresh braids and moved with pride. While Graham spoke on the phone to Jackie, the three of us arrogantly leaned on my car as a crew of campus girls passed us by and commented on our resemblance of a broke R&B group. Lydea called me the same moment that Cassell and Graham countered by snapping on how dreadful they looked.

"Hey, Jay, I'm leaving my room soon," my girl said. "You wanna meet me out front in a few minutes?"

"Consider it done. I'm on my way." I hung up and began to reach for my door handle. "Aight, fellas. Leave them girls alone. It's time. Yo slim, where's your girl at, man?" I directed at Graham. "Lydea's ready before Jackie? What?"

"Whatever, dude," he said, brushing his shoulders off. "My girl's putting on her lipstick. Pop your locks, while I pop my collar."

"Don't get too comfortable in that seat either. You and *lipstick girl* will be in the back; Lyd has shotgun. Yo, Cassell!" I yelled. "You good?"

"Yes, sir!" he shouted back, role-playing a chauffeur by opening his car door for himself.

Moments later, we pulled along the sidewalk near Lydea's dormitory as she wittingly moved like a runway model towards my car, adorned with matching white blossoms in her hair.

"Graham, don't get up," Lydea said closing his door, as I got out to meet her. "I'll sit in the back with Jackie."

"Are you sure?" I asked, receiving a firm kiss to my surprised lips. "Well there it is!" I chivalrously shut her door. "Let's roll!"

Soon after scooping up Jackie, the group of us arrived at the popular steak house and was seated shortly after. The second our waitress took our orders, Cassell looked at me, and I looked at Graham. We checked our watches and nodded in agreement. Suspiciously, the three of us stood up from the table and left the ladies puzzled.

"Hey!" Jackie projected, looking very nice despite her braces. "Where y'all going?"

"We'll be back," Cassell said, as we all looked at her.

"I swear, y'all better not do anything crazy," Lydea warned, fixing her lengthy earrings. "I mean it."

As calm as could be, we stepped out the lobby doors and then trotted wildly to the back of the parking lot, opposite of where I had parked, in order to get the wrapped flowers from Cassell's car. Slick, huh? Our plan was seconds away from unraveling. We retrieved our roses and Cassell went back inside to join the girls. Graham and I remained in the parking lot to rehearse our artful routine. Once we found harmony in our practiced steps, we returned to the main entrance.

"They're gonna be so embarrassed," I said, anxiously.

"Yeah, and we 'bouta look like some idiots," Graham agreed. "This feels great. I love it!"

With the two of us as excited as ever, we busted through the double doors. All of a sudden, the lobby area felt noticeably larger than before. We held our half dozen, long stem pink roses in our right arms, tucked like a football. We positioned our shoulders side-by-side and moved forward, in sync, throughout the restaurant. I added a smooth bop to my step, which gave my body language the freedom to holler out, *Hey, everybody! Stop what you're doing and watch this.*

From a distance, I stared at Lydea sitting at the table as she stared back. Her mouth was wide open from disbelief. Once Graham and I got close enough, we came to a halt. In our best singing voices, we sang, "I-I-I only have eyeees foooor youuuu!"

My hands shook from the impulse. Our gesture made our ladies gleam with delight. I leaned over to hand Lydea her flowers and kissed her blushed left cheek. "I love you, girl," I whispered, hearing multiple tables clap for us.

While my face was close to hers, she whispered back, "How did I know you were gonna do something crazy like this? I know you too well, Jay. And that's why I love you too," she said returning the kiss.

"I'm glad I'm single!" Cassell shouted, leaning back in his chair, bringing laughter to our surrounding tables.

Time flew by and the dinner went well. We ate and laughed. In between the laughter, we ate some more. Following our random group pictures, we left the restaurant for our next destination, the Alpha ball. The heavy food gave us a warm feeling below that took away all urges to immediately dance, so Lydea and I spent the first hour mingling while we waited for our food to settle.

Similar to the formal dance on the Spirit of Norfolk Cruise months before, wild college students filled the dance floor. The Alphas stomped their way through the large crowd as the DJ hyped up their routine. The oversized speakers gave a booming sound to the old school hip-hop music. My feet wanted to move to the tempo like everyone else; instead I stood behind my sweet-smelling lady, holding her waist tight, moving everything but my feet.

"Yo, I thought all Latin American girls like to dance."

"We do," she replied, "but you're not ready."

"I am. I really am," I pushed. "C'mon, Lyd."

"Na, na, na. Right here's fine."

"Aight, well start moving these hips then." I gripped tighter. "I feel like dancing, girl! Let's dance!"

Trying to get Lydea on the dance floor was a challenge. I accepted the fact that she wasn't the undignified dancer that I was hoping she would be. Nevertheless, we remained stationed along the perimeter of the wooden area and enjoyed the rhythm of the night. Cassell, on the other hand, danced out of control with three beautiful ladies around him.

"Yo, Jay, I could stay here all night, baby!" he yelled over the loud music, looking tipsy.

"I feel you, dog!" I shouted back, spotting Graham and Jackie on the other side, having fun as well, switching partners.

The night ended with one hit song after the other. Being the photogenic type of guy that I am, I clicked away at our special moments to cherish them for years to come.

Breakdown

When the weather was good, there wasn't too much that could take away our happiness. The sunshine warmed up our lives and produced a ray of light that made us grin from the inside out. Lydea and I were at peace when we had fun together. The night of the Alpha ball was a field goal in my book. Throw your hands up! It's good!

I love getting dressed up, looking like the Southern old-school playa or the Italian gangsta. Or better yet, the clean-cut guy in church who never has a bad Sunday. It felt twice as good having an attractive lady on my arm. She made me feel like a movie star. Having a dream girl by my side had always been a secret longing of mine and Lydea was that. She was my pride and joy. She was my self-esteem. She became my motivation for waking up every morning. Why I felt like that, I will never know. It was like she became an idol.

~ *It's Raining* ~

20

By this time, the month of May had arrived and my 22nd birthday was days away. For some sinful reason, I had the craving to repeat the same action that took place on my 20th. The truth was, I still hadn't removed the unrighteous traditional ways of enjoying them with my significant others. So, without jumping into too many details, the same occurrence happened again. The Friday before my birthday, my lady and I found ourselves in her dorm, practicing our bad habit. When all the fun and games were finished, we rested in each other's arms. No television. No radio. Only our soft voices were heard.

"Let's stay together," I told her.

"What?" Lydea responded. "This summer?"

"Yeah. This summer. I want us to stay together."

"Really? Me too! Why do you have to leave at all?" she asked with her head relaxed on my chest.

"I wanna make your pops proud," I said, running my fingers through her hair. "Oh, and speaking of your pops, he called me this morning."

"No, he didn't," she said with her eyes slightly closed.

"Yes, he did," I corrected. "It was like six this morning when he called. I was dead asleep, of course, but he said that your phone was off and my number was the next one he had."

"If it was that early, then he was on his way to work. What did he want? He's probably wondering about my scholarship money."

"Who knows? He never said. I asked him if you were going home for the summer and he acted like I never asked a question. He's definitely a man of few words, that's for sure."

"Mmm hmm. That's my wonderful father."

"Is he always like that or is it 'cause I'm a stranger?" I asked, still replaying our naughtiness in my mind.

"It's not you. Believe me. He's been that way since I was little. My father grew up in Venezuela, so being seen and not heard is all he knows. He's a man of silence."

"That's rough."

"Please. He hasn't sent me money since February. That's rough," she complained, covered in her soft fuchsia blanket. "The last time we spoke, he kept saying, 'Grow up. Be independent.' But Jay, tell me how am I supposed to be who he wants me to be if he's a terrible father figure?" My lady sat up. "And to make matters worse, this father of mine has yet to ask me to join him this summer. It's like his home is off-limits to me."

"He tried to call you this morning, girl," I reminded.

"Okay and where's his message?" she said, laying back down, releasing a heavy breath.

"Well, have you spoken with your Uncle Carlos? What about your Aunt Claire?" I wondered.

"Yeah, of course I did. My uncle said he's selling his house in a few weeks and will be moving in with his fiancée." Lydea grunted in frustration, squeezing her pillow. "And my aunt's going back to South America for most of the summer. I don't care anymore. I'll just be homeless."

"For real, where are you gonna stay?" I said seriously. "They're kickin' folks out next week."

"Jay, I don't know. This is so stressful. I hate my family."

"You don't hate your family. Don't say that."

"They're never there for me," she said, covering her face with her violet pillow. "My own father doesn't care."

"You want me to talk with him?" I offered, still brainstorming different options.

"No. Don't worry," she muffled. I pulled the pillow from her face as she continued, "It'll work out. If anything, Jason said I could stay with him until my folks take me in."

I sat there, looking at the shape of her figure underneath the thin blanket that covered her. In the back of my mind, I screamed, *Lord, say this isn't going to happen again.* How could I remain her boyfriend, being in Atlanta, knowing that she'd be with her kryptonite? I had to get her to New Jersey, one way or another.

We quarreled on the best alternative, yet her final decision ended right back at Jason's place. She sat up again and positioned herself against the wall, next to me. "Jay, do you really love me?" she said intertwining her legs with mine.

"Do I really love you? Lyd, I wouldn't say it if I didn't mean it. Do you really love me?" I threw it back.

"You know I love you. I just get scared sometimes."

"Scared? What's to be scared of?" I asked, reaching for her hands. "Don't be scared. I'm not a monster."

"I know you're not. I'm afraid that you're gonna leave again." Lydea turned to face me. "And I *know* I'm not the best girlfriend in the world. You deserve so much better than me. I mean, I have a lot of flaws and personal issues I need to work on. Plus the fact that I—"

"Hey," I said, cutting her short. "I'm not perfect either. We all got flaws, somewhere. Some more than others, of course, but still, look at me. I'll be twenty-two on Monday and I still can't grow sideburns," I joked, turning her frown into a smile.

"Whatever, boy. You have a baby face. Your flaws are different than mine." She gazed at the ceiling, as if her heart needed to confess something. A wave of stillness filled the room. Her gaze remained.

"Babe, you all right?" I asked.

"Jay, if I tell you something, will you promise to not get mad?" she asked. I leisurely untangled my legs from hers, pretending to be deaf, reaching for my shirt.

"Hey, did you hear me?"

"Huh?"

"I need to get something off my chest," she said, twisting around, still hardly dressed. "But before I tell you, promise me that you won't get mad."

"Lydea! I won't get mad," I said madly, pulling my crushed yellow Polo shirt over my wifebeater. "I didn't get mad last time, did I? Just say what you gotta say."

"You know what…forget it." She reached over me for her hairbrush on the desk. "You're already angry. I'll tell you another time."

"C'mon, man, just tell me. It can't be that bad, right?" I pushed, trying to get the story out of her. "Was it something that happened yesterday? Today? What?"

"Well, not really. A lil' further back then yesterday. Ugh," she exhaled. "Let me just tell you. But don't get mad, all right?"

"Aight. Dang. What happened already?"

"The day I brought you food in the Tech Building, Jason had dropped me off on campus, and…he did it again."

"Did what again?" I said sharply.

"Well, when I was getting out his car, before I could even shut the door, he shouted, 'Oh, so I can't get a kiss good-bye?' and I looked at him like he had lost his mind. Then he was like, 'After all I've done for you. We're supposed to be best friends,' blah, blah, blah. 'Just gimme a quick one right here,' and he pointed to his cheek," Lydea quoted him. My eyes drifted around the room while she spoke. My eyelid began to twitch in anger. She went on. "So I leaned over the passenger seat to give him an innocent, friendly kiss on his cheek and he jerked his head around and kissed me on my lips. That's when I pushed his face away and slammed the door. He tricked me again so he could kiss me," she brutally explained. "Sorry I took my anger out on you."

I sat on the edge of her messy bed, flabbergasted, experiencing emptiness like never before. I was emotionally dead. My mind had left minutes ago. Out of the abundance of my heart, my mouth spoke.

"That has gotta be the dumbest thing I've ever heard," I said sadly, searching for answers to feed my lack of understanding. Another 20 minutes went by before I made my way to the parking lot.

"Jayden, are you okay? You haven't said much. You're not mad at me, are you?" she wondered, while I looked for my parents' '82 hooptie that I used as transportation that day due to my own car trouble. "Please don't be mad.

I didn't do anything wrong this time. I wanna be honest with you, like you asked me to be. No more secrets, right?" She stood next to the driver's door and watched me remove the keys from my pocket. "Look, I know it's late. I don't want to hold you up. Call me when you get home, okay?"

I opened the door and sat down, avoiding all hugs or kisses good-bye. "Yeah, I'll call you," I mumbled, spotting an unattractive couple happily walking to their car.

"I love you," Lydea said faintly, awaiting my response. She shut my prehistoric car door and stepped back to watch me putter off. Showing no feelings, I drove through the security gate and pulled out my phone to delete her number. Who was I kidding? That wasn't her number in the first place, and it surely wasn't her phone. I gripped my steering wheel with my left hand, grinding my molars together, remembering that Jason had their phone for the weekend. I scrolled through my text messages and opened the last one I had received from Lydea. It consisted of three words that she proclaimed often: I Love U. Driving in fury, I hit reply and aimed a short message Jason's way. "She's all yours. I'm thru."

Moments later, the expressway traffic came to a sudden halt. I waited near the tunnel in a sea of brake lights, calling out to God in repentance. "My Lord, my Lord, forgive my sinful ways," I prayed. "Please forgive me," I begged, hoping that God could be merciful towards my practice of fornication and utter rebellion. The entire ride home, I drove overwhelmed with guilt and shame as my blurry vision barely returned me to Newport News safely. Within my mind, I deleted Lydea's title. She was no longer my girl.

Breakdown

Confusion, sorrow, grief, pain, depression, regret, agony, suffering, anger, rage, weakness, disappointment, uncertainty, distress, anguish, demise, insult, disgust, self-pity, misery, humiliation, and any other terrible feeling you can think of belongs on this page.

I reached my house and I was mentally single again. Lydea and I had been together for nearly seven months and this was our fourth breakup! She was oblivious to this one though. She had no clue that I had removed myself from the picture. This breakup was unspoken; my body language had said it all. The disappointment in my eyes should've told her that we were finished. Lydea should've realized once she chose to hit me with her honest surprise that it would lead to another "Bye-bye, so long, I can't do this anymore, sorry it didn't work out" speech.

It began to rain in my life once more. This time the hard falling raindrops were leaving scars. Emotionally, I was soaking wet. I was weighed down and saturated by my burdensome clothes. Lydea and I were finished—again.

~ *Where's My Umbrella?* ~

21

The following day, I was at work, but my mind had traveled elsewhere. During my 15 minute break, I checked my phone and noticed a few missed phone calls and a voice message. It was Lydea. I listened to her speak. "Jayden, why didn't you call me when you got home last night? I stayed up until two in the morning. And why was your phone off when I called? I was worried. Don't make me worry, okay? I care about you too much. Anyways, I know you get off at six. I'll get Jason to drive me to your job so I can see you. I hope you're not mad from last night. You sure didn't say much when you left. Oh well, I'm talking too much. Call me when you can, okay? Bye."

Her Latin tone was regular. No enthusiasm or fast speech, just her normal voice. I didn't think twice about calling her back. I simply deleted the message and continued on my break. I went back to my register and tended to the customers as before. Three more hours zoomed by and I was now looking forward to clocking out for the night.

I stood at the register farthest from the entrance while the customers scattered about. I felt the vibration of my phone in my pocket as another voice message was left. It was time for me to count down my drawer, but there wasn't a manager in sight. To add to my impatience, I watched an elderly couple push a cart full of items right up to my register. I greeted them with a cheerful smile and began to ring them up. Halfway finished with their purchase, my eyes recognized a familiar face in the distance. A rough, Timberland-boot, Phillies baseball-cap-wearing hoodlum was headed in my direction. My enemy was walking on the grounds of my territory. *Sound the alarm!* my mind screamed. *Where's Lydea? What does he want?* The closer Jason got to my register, the faster the adrenaline rushed through my veins. My customers became invisible. Everything moved in slow motion. My thoughts flared out of control. If he wanted to fight me, then I was more than ready. My inner strength was growing. I had enough power to manhandle a raging bull. My heart began pounding. I was prepared to react to his slightest move. We hadn't seen eye-to-eye since the first mishap and there he was, pacing towards me. *I wish he would,* my conscience repeated.

As I stood facing the elderly couple, he yeilded to my left with a burning cigarette in his mouth. "Yo," his urban voice projected, receiving the attention of my customers. I turned around, holding my right fist, low and tight. "This is from Lydea," he added, holding a letter between his fingers. I saw his relaxed demeanor and instantly my built-up tension vanished. I reached for the letter as he dropped it in my hand. He then casually walked away towards the exit doors. Before I knew it, he was gone.

"Sorry about that," I said, refocusing my attention back on to the couple as they awaited their total. "Your total is $84.37. Do you need help with the fish tank, sir?"

"No, thank you, young man. I can get it," the balding gentleman said with confidence as his wife handed me a check.

"Fred, let this nice young man help you," she insisted as he pushed the shopping cart to leave.

"Thelma, I told him, no thank you. I got it. Now, grab the receipt from him before we leave it."

"Oops." She covered her mouth. I smiled and handed it to her. "God bless you, young man."

My disoriented manager appeared the same moment the couple moseyed along. "All right slick," he said, turning off my register light with his soiled, untucked shirt. "Let's get you counted down. Charity should be in shortly. That girl's always late. Have you noticed?"

"Yeah, but you gotta admit, Stan, she is a hard worker. Plus she has like three jobs," I said, gathering my loose currency.

"Well, if she had *two* jobs, then she could get to work on time and maybe even get a raise," my manager said as we paced to the front office, dodging the swinging tail of an energetic all black German Shepherd.

I quickly counted down my drawer and entered it into the system. I was still shaken up from the boxing match that could've taken place. Afterwards, I hurried off to the break room and ripped open the note. I sat down and read it word-for-word. The letter started with Lydea giving excuses about not wanting to come in and disrupt my job. She babbled on about how she'd be waiting in the parking lot for me when I got off. Before my eyes could reach the end of the teal-pigmented paper, my assistant manager walked into the break room, straightening her thick glasses. "Hey, Jay-Rock, would you mind staying another hour or two? Charity called out. We need another cashier up front."

I juggled the question in my head. "That's cool," I said with a willing attitude, knowing that Lydea and Jason were outside waiting for me. "I get time and a half for staying late, right?" I joked as I slipped past her, tucking my letter away.

"Thanks for staying," she said, trailing behind me. "Time and a half, I don't think so. But I'll see what I can do to compensate you."

For the next hour, I worked the register and kept the lines moving. When I finally clocked out, I left the store and scanned the parking lot in every direction, searching for Jason's burgundy Cadillac. While thunder was clearly heard, lightening was absent, and so were Lydea and Jason.

Later, while I ate dinner with my family, the ringing of my phone sounded in the distance. I got up and glanced at the "unavailable" caller ID that appeared. I let it finish ringing and soon after, it rang again. I peeked at the number and simply ignored Jason's digits. Minutes later, it rang again. If it wasn't a call, then it was a text message. My phone was constantly making noise. Lydea wrote remorseful text messages, explaining how sorry she was. My voicemail recorded her whimpering and pleading with a hurting heart for me to answer her calls. She received no sympathy from me.

It was now a quarter to midnight and my phone was still a hotline. I can't count the number of missed phone calls. A plethora of calls would be a good way to translate it. I became professionally stubborn. I didn't pick up once. The time had me wondering why she was still calling from his phone and not from her dorm. On Saturdays, I usually expected her back on campus no later than 10 p.m.. I was concerned, but my stone-like heart fought the urge to care.

I sat on my bed with the lights out and stared at the cell phone in my palm. I still had nothing to say to her a whole day later. Many minutes had gone by since the last call, and then suddenly my phone rang again. I let it ring. Eventually I checked the voicemail that was left and the automated machine said I had eight new messages. I pressed the phone close to my ear and listened to Lydea's words go from uncontrollable screaming, to violent cussing, to a calm cry. The many heartbreaking messages that she left said that Jason was trying to rape her. The fear in her voice was proof that things had gotten grim. Rape was a little too severe of a crime for me to acknowledge, but I paid close attention to her every spoken word. In Lydea's final message, she asked one question that echoed in my mind for the night, "Why didn't you come and get me?" she sobbed.

I deleted all my messages, cut my phone off and collapsed on my pillow. My spirit was dry. I attempted to take my situation before the Lord, but before I could even spill my heart to him, I was fast asleep.

Sunday morning in church, I sat on the same predictable pew with my family. At the end of the sermon, our pastor asked for all eyes to be closed and heads to be bowed. My troubles and burdens bubbled out of me like a mixture of vinegar and baking soda. I heard my spirit weeping out loud. Where was my umbrella when I needed it? Several ladies sitting nearby laid their hands on my back, as my tears became a downpour.

Breakdown

Where do tears come from? If I were to become bruised and battered, yes, tears would appear due to the throbbing physical pain. If I received news that a close relative or friend suddenly passed away, yes, I would probably cry. If I graduated from college and conquered a childhood of poverty, yes, I would shed a tear due to the joyous feeling of accomplishment and purpose. Standing at the altar in all white with my soon-to-be wife, whom I love with strength, I will probably cry. Kneeling next to the hospital bed, cradling our first child, yes, I will cry; expressing my gratitude to God and God alone. In my mind, when a man cries, he exposes his weaknesses, which is ultimately his strength.

The book of Genesis records that Joseph, a vessel of God, cried often (Gen. 43:30; 45:1, 2, 14, 15; 46:29; 50:1, 17). His soft heart towards his brothers brought tears that were much different than mine. Scripture states that King David watered his couch with tears (Psalms 6:6). In John 11:35, which is the shortest and one of the most powerful verses in the Bible, it says, "*Jesus wept.*" What does it actually take for Jesus to cry? That verse has such an impact on me. That Sunday morning, when the tears rained from my eyes, it was purely my outlet of expression. The average person didn't know my pain, but Jesus knew. Only Jesus and I really knew.

~ *Where's Her Umbrella?* ~

22

That Monday, the day of my birthday, it literally rained non-stop in the city of Norfolk. I remember trucking through the puddle-filled parking lot first thing that morning to meet up with my classmates in the library to review our upcoming Chemistry final. The six of us sat around a table for four and discussed our exam.

"Aight, y'all, I'm bouncin'," Graham said, standing up a while later, ruining our pity party.

"Why?" I questioned, as we all looked at him.

"Man, we ain't studying. We're complaining. We're whining over a test that *none* of us are gonna pass."

"Oh, I'm *gonna* pass," I said with optimism. "Me, you, and the Chemistry Crew. We got this, G. Sit back down."

"Nah, I'm good. I'm glad to see you're so positive about it, Jay. Maybe if I'm lucky, there'll be a seat diagonally behind you with my name on it."

"Bump that. We pulled that stunt our freshman year, man. I ain't helping you cheat anymore. I'm tryin' to graduate. You feel me?"

"I know that's right," the others agreed, bumping fists with me.

"Man, it's whatever," Graham said walking away. "Come Wednesday, I'll be looking for that seat. Oh yeah," he ran back, "Jay, I almost forgot. Pray for me, bruh. Right now. I gotta ten o'clock Calculus exam that I gotta pass."

"Dang dude, you need prayer?" a classmate asked.

"Heck yeah! If y'all think Chemistry is hard, sit in my math class for five minutes. I'm gettin' an anxiety attack just thinkin' about it. But for real," he added, leaning over the table in surrender, "I need God to help me pass my final."

"Aight, fellas. Let's do this. Everybody bow your heads," I said right then, receiving strange looks from my colleagues. "Yo, everybody bow your heads," I repeated, ready to pray. "Lord, we thank you for brother Graham," I said as they all joined in. "Please be with him as he takes his Calculus exam. Supernaturally give him the right answers. And Lord, be with the rest of us throughout this exam week as well. Your grace is sufficient. We ask these things in Jesus' name. A to the man."

"Yes!" Graham rejoiced, standing up. "That's what I needed. Thanks, Jay. I owe you one."

"Ayo, tomorrow—same time, same place," one of the guys yelled as G raised his arm in agreement, shuffling away. Minutes later, the rest of us gathered our items and left the table, still laughing at our chubby friend.

While the pack of us marched down the stairs, I hid amongst the shoulders of my taller friends in case Lydea happened to pass us. What did she expect me to say if I saw her, "Hi"?

My crew halted by the sliding glass exit doors along with random students, and watched the heavy rain descend sideways. The Lord must've ordained my timing, because the same ex-girlfriend that I was trying to duck came shuffling through the entrance doors, as wet as could be. Lydea caught eyes with me from under her hoodie and she boldly approached. "We need to talk."

I glanced at my boys standing next to me, while Lydea swiftly walked towards the stairwell. "Jayden, you better go handle dat," they said, snickering.

"Man, shut up," I forced through my teeth, following her up the stairs. She dropped her bag onto the table and pulled her chair out. My actions mirrored hers.

"Why didn't you answer your phone this weekend?" she asked with a deadly look.

"I had nothin' to say to you," I respectfully answered. "Where's your umbrella?"

"It's broken," she said removing her hoodie. "Do you have any idea what I've been through? Do you even care?"

I sat there rubbing my eyes, trying hard to remain planted on the inside, yet still look concerned. "I heard your messages," I said with a straight face. "I read your texts."

"Do you know what happened to me, Jayden? No, you don't. You'll never know what happened because you weren't there!" Her words spoke to my heart. "All I've ever wanted was for you to be there for me, and this is how I get treated?"

"Hold up. My question to you is—why were you calling me from your boy's phone Saturday night? Not once did you call me from your room phone."

"You wouldn't have answered anyways!" Lydea said, heated, scanning the area. "If you'd like to know why I wasn't in my room, you can ask. The *reason* is because he wouldn't drop me back at school, thank you very much. I said that already in the messages. I needed you to get me, but you never picked up your stupid phone."

"Oh, so now it's my fault?" I argued, sitting across from her for the first time since last semester.

"Why is it when I call Jason, he's there for me?" she challenged. "When my mom passed away and no one helped me cope, he was there. When I was depressed, he was there. Jayden, I called you so many times this weekend and you didn't answer once! Why can't I ever rely on you? What did I do so wrong?"

I absorbed it all in, listening to Lydea express herself. I couldn't understand how she could still say Jason's name in a positive light if what happened was true. How could she even call this guy her best friend? How could she justify being friends with a person who curses at her and takes advantage of her weaknesses? She was entangled in a soul-tie that I hadn't been introduced to.

Due to my 11 a.m. exam that was approaching, the both of us left the library. We walked out into the drizzling rain like an estranged couple. I kept a distance between us, still not admitting that I was no longer her man. Lydea trailed me through the soggy weather into the Technology Building, wanting to talk. My fast steps must've given light to our status.

"Take me back!" she shouted, jumping in front of me on the middle landing of the stairway with her displaced hair and smeared eyeliner. "Jayden, don't do this to me. I love you. Take me back. I promise I'll change."

I stood there and looked like the complete opposite of her. *Oh how the tables have turned,* I thought to myself, glancing into her weary eyes. I then reflected on the words I wrote months ago when she sat next to me on the bus ride from New York:

> *My page is dry and my pen is wet*
> *I'm standing at the bottom of a flight of stairs*
> *And all I can do is take baby steps*
> *I need to let my lady rest*
> *I wish I could take away my lady's stress*
> *But guess what?*
> *That's not a problem for me to take away*
> *I have to remind myself everyday*

From our trip up north to that moment in the stairwell, my feelings hadn't changed. After disputing, I dismissed myself from her presence. I walked into my classroom and glanced back at her standing in the hall. Similar to a young toddler carelessly dragging her rag doll with scarlet pigtails on the ground, Lydea dragged her broken spirit. Hours went by and shockingly enough, by late afternoon, her room number showed up on my caller ID.

"Hello," I answered.

"Hey, um, you can expect a call from Jason soon."

"Why?" I raised my tone.

"He said that he wants to talk with you."

"Are you playin' with me? What's he gotta say?"

"Jayden, I don't know. I'm just letting you know that he's going to call you, okay?" she said in a tranquil voice.

I gave a heavy breath. "Aight. Fine. Bye."

I hated the idea of him calling me. I left the third floor of the Tech Building and descended to the first. I posted outside of the computer lab, along the corridor wall, awaiting Jason's call. I dreaded hearing him speak, especially when his words were aimed at me. As expected, my phone rang.

"Yo," I hesitantly answered.

"Yo, Jayden. This is Jason. Can you talk?" he said in his monotone city voice.

"Yeah, I'm good," I mumbled.

"Aight, well, I was talking with Lyd a lil' while ago and she sounded pitiful, man. You know she really loves you, right?" he liberally said as I leaned against the wall, still confused as to why I even answered the phone. I agreed as he rambled on. "You're the only one she ever talks about. This weekend she was so messed up because you weren't there for her. Yo, for real, I wish she cared for me as much as she cares about you."

"You know what, I'm glad you brought that up," I responded as my heart rate increased. "Lydea left me dozens of messages Saturday night crying and screaming as you yelled in the background for her to get off the phone. Answer this, you sick punk!" I shouted into the phone, changing our serenity into an uproar. "Did you touch my girl?"

"What? Is this what you wanna talk about? What if I did, huh? What the hell you gonna do? I'm tryin' to help you right now, sucker. Don't flip this back on me," Jason spit back.

"I don't believe this trash. I don't even know why I answered. Don't *ever* touch my girl again."

"Oh so *now* she's your girl?" he provoked, right before I hung up in his ear. How dare he try to coach me on working things out with the same girl that he wanted for himself? I crept back upstairs to the AutoCAD Lab and looked over my senior project with my mind in a frenzy.

Later that day, I noticed Lydea out of the corner of my eye, standing outside of the lab doors, unannounced, clutching a small bag spilling with items. I slid out into the hall and positioned myself in front of her.

"What's all this?"

"Here. These are yours," she said, handing me the bag.

"What are you talking about?" I sifted through it. "This stuff ain't mine; it's yours. These cards, teddy bears, deflated balloons. This is all yours. Lyd, I gave you all this. This is your watch from our sixth-month anniversary."

"Take it," she insisted with watery eyes. "It's yours now. I have no use for things that have no meaning."

"Why can't you keep it?" I asked, resting the bag on my shoes. "And I know you're not giving me back the heart pillow I gave you. It was your Valentine's gift. I ain't taking that back. It's *yours*."

"Whatever you've given me, I don't want anymore," she made clear.

We stood in the hall, clashing, as my pleasant friend, Chelsea, turned the corner holding four helium-filled birthday balloons for me. But she quickly got the picture.

"You can put those down right there, sweetie." Lydea pointed, with flames in her eyes. "He ain't your man."

"Thanks, Chelsea." I awkwardly grinned, moving my feet from under the bag. "Right there is fine."

"Okay," she said embarrassed, turning back around. "Happy birthday, Jay."

"And you get mad over Jason?" Lydea shouted at me. "What's her problem? Why she gotta do all that?"

"Are you jealous?" I jabbed. "Tell me if you are."

"Over her? A freshman? Far from jealous, alright."

"Good. So stop acting like you are."

"I'm not!"

"Yo, you know what the difference is between Jason and Chelsea?"

"I don't care, but I'm sure you're gonna tell me."

"Yeah, I am. It's the time they *actually* spend with us," I said. "Plus Chelsea and I don't have a past. You and your boy do."

"Whatever," she disagreed. "I've read several notes from off your car that you'll never see. I know she wants you."

"Stop throwing her in the mix, Lyd! We don't have a past and we don't have a present. I call her my friend and mean it. You shouldn't care if she likes me. I don't mess with the girl. Period."

After exchanging words, I gathered my backpack from the classroom. The two of us eventually made it downstairs and walked through the gray and misty weather.

"You just don't get it, do you?" she spoke with her hands. "I already told you that I don't like that boy. I feel nothing for him. At times, I even hate him, but he's all I have. What do you want me to do? I have no one else. Both of my parents are gone in my mind, so who do I really have if you leave me?"

"I don't know," I shrugged.

"Jayden, don't make Jason all I have. I don't want him. I want you," she said hitting me. "I want you!"

"Will you stop?" I yelled, grabbing her swinging forearm. "You don't want me. You don't."

"I do! Just take me back. I promise I won't hurt you ever again. Take me back. I promise!" she pleaded, following me to my car, which was parked many yards away.

"You've said all this already. You've promised me before," I said to her. "You've broken your promises too many times. You're simply repeating broken promises."

"Just listen. I can't let you leave me. I don't have any one else. Jayden, I love you! Don't you love me?" She paused, caught her question in midair and milked it to death, tugging on my sleeve. "Don't you still love me? Tell me you still love me. Just Friday we made love and you said it. Tell me that you love me again, please. Say it once more. Baby, I love you. I need you. Tell me you love me."

Her words strummed my emotions, yet I was determined to remain strong. Lydea begged until her crying became undignified. I had never seen a girl cry over me for a complete day like she had. I persisted to get into my car and out of the rain. It was difficult to leave her standing there, but I had to do it. I drove away, tardy for my birthday dinner with my family, looking at her in my rearview mirror, kneeling on the pavement, crying under her hoodie. The day I turned 22 was like none other.

Breakdown

I awaited a new season and a fresh start with the Lord. I was excited to see what God had in store for me. A breath of fresh air is what I'd call it. I was letting bygones-be-bygones. I was closing the door to the past and opening one for the future. I didn't deserve the pain that I was given, intentional or not.

If my pain felt the way that it did, then I'm sure Lydea's was doubled. Her situation didn't have a clear-cut equation, and that's what made it so difficult to solve. I glimpsed at the soul inside of her, crying and yearning for a strong base in her life. The tears that streamed from her attractive eyes weren't from me walking away from my role of being her man, but something much deeper. She wanted a foundation. She wanted love and stability. Those were two values that I was able and ready to give; yet I chose not to. That night, I stooped by my bedside and prayed for her longer than I prayed for myself.

~ *Jayden's Lyric* ~

23

I began to observe Lydea and Jason's friendship again. So, in order to truly see things as they did, I had to remove myself from myself and put on their shoes. It was shocking to me that his shoes were easier to fill than hers. Despite living opposite lives, Jason and I actually related in more ways than I thought. We were two struggling college students searching for identity through love.

Jason wasn't known for his handsome features, yet Lydea being called beautiful gave him all the confidence he needed. Watching them walk together forced me to view them as beauty and the beast. However, she was my beauty, not his. By Lydea claiming Jason as her best friend, it made him feel like a king. But once I stepped on to the scene, his manhood was challenged. I took his trophy. The best friend who he claimed, I made mine.

A specific song grabbed my thoughts when I viewed life through his eyes. "Half Crazy" is the title and it's performed by one of my favorite male R&B artists, Musiq Soulchild. I fell in love with this song when it first blazed the radio. After listening to the words and applying them to my circumstance, I actually thought Jason might've written the lyrics. It's amazing how well it tells their story.

He had an obsession, a fight within. It was obvious. I asked myself, mentally stomping around in his Timberland boots, *Why hasn't he backed off yet? He's missing something, something from within. I'm positive.* My conclusion was that Jason had a foundation full of cracks. This alone will lead any young man or woman in search of stability or, even more so, the first sign of love. He wanted to love her, but he couldn't. It was then that I understood his anger and realized what it's like to want to love someone and not have that love returned. Truthfully, I didn't have to put on his shoes to know that feeling. This obsessive kind of love for someone can very well lead to rape and physical abuse. At that point, I had to take his shoes off and promise myself to never put them on again. I couldn't relate to that part of him. The devil had a hold on him, which had a hold on Lydea, who had a hold on me. It was a strong hold that I had to break.

Fitting into Lydea's shoes was a struggle. How could I get to know the real person if she didn't even know who the real person was that lived inside of her? On one hand, she gave me praise for being the only true friend who could understand her, while her other hand was busy hitting me. Were my gracious ways really a good thing? They seemed to benefit me so poorly.

Lydea's view on love was unclear. It was difficult for her to present it to me the same way that I was taught to present it to others. I realized that her shoes didn't fit my feet either, so they didn't stay on long. The one thing I realized when I wore them was this: I couldn't give her what she sincerely needed. Only Jesus could completely heal her heart, mind, soul, and spirit. If I was the vessel sent to position her in front of Jesus, then I was falling extremely short.

I remember when "Me, Myself and I," a heartfelt song by the R&B diva, Beyonce, hit the airwaves. The meaning behind the song's lyrics magically removed the scales from my eyes. It was true; I had to become my own best friend. If I expected my girl to always be there for me, to keep it real with me, to edify me, and to have my back when I needed her to, then I'd be one very disappointed young man. However, with the help of the Holy Spirit, I could be self-obedient, self-disciplined, self-encouraged, self-critical, and live with self-esteem all the days of my life. Me, myself, and God was all I needed in the end.

By the end of the spring semester there was a song by the music superstar, Usher that was setting car speakers on fire. College students drove by blaring it with the assurance that this was the jam. Girls strolled to class, humming the tune out loud. Guys began breaking girls' hearts, telling them, "Let it burn." No one, except maybe Usher felt the lyrics the same way that I did. The first half of the song was like my words to Lydea and the second half of the song was like her words to me.

The day after my birthday, the two of us ended up on the second floor of the library at the same hour. She stood amongst a small crowd of guys, laughing as I sat at my table studying. She slowly approached. "Jayden, have you thought about us?" she wondered, still stuck on reconciliation.

"Lydea," I said, with my eyes in my textbook, "just let it burn. I'm not involved anymore." She stormed away, but little did she know, I was burning on the inside as well.

During those spring months, another song by Mario Winans, an R&B singer, had received much airplay on the radio. This was one of those tunes that could get stuck in your head, and before you realized it, you're humming the melody all afternoon. "I Don't Wanna Know" was the name of this song, and it seemed like every urban radio station in Hampton Roads had it in rotation. The lyrics describe the artist not wanting to know the truth about what's really going on with his cheating girlfriend. Every time he would look into her eyes, he knew there was a hidden truth that he didn't want to hear. One morning, this song woke me up through my clock radio and the lyrics hit me like a ton of bricks. I listened to the words while resting in bed and compared them to my situation. I too, didn't want to know what went on during those weekends when Lydea and Jason hung out together. I didn't want to hear the truth that she hid in her mouth, yet I needed to. It's divine how a simple song can be so relative to one person but be so irrelevant to the next.

Breakdown

Music is such a beautiful language of expression, would you agree? Blending the words of a song with a soft background instrument can be so spirit-lifting when played right. Have you ever felt the relaxing combination of a talented pianist and a graceful vocalist? Have you been privileged enough to hear a seasoned guitarist strum the strings with emotion, joined by a passionate crooner? Have you ever heard a soloist or a choir flutter their octaves with precision while a rhythmic drummer held the tempo? The professional arrangement of music and lyrics is indescribable. I felt like Lydea and I were the combination of such when we walked in harmony. Once in a blue moon a love song was recorded by the two of us. We were like a walking soundtrack. But when the soundtrack of our relationship wasn't spinning right, our ears could hear the scratches. Due to our status being deleted at the time, no music was heard at all. As a result, emotional stumbling blocks such as loneliness and gloom were thrown in my path. Yet, in time, those same stumbling blocks became my steppingstones. God's guidance became my dance steps.

~ Promises ~

24

In my solitude, I fought with myself. I tried to keep my ex-girlfriend out of my mind. This was the longest breakup she and I had experienced, and it felt like the worst. For some reason, after all that we had been through, I was still being pulled towards her. My heart was confused.

The next day at NNU, I was prepared to give my senior project presentation. Although Lydea and I weren't on the best of terms, I anticipated her attendance. To my surprise, while I set up the hardware, she quietly snuck through the rear door of the classroom and slouched low in her seat, camouflaged amongst the other students. I smiled.

Regardless of our status, she was still my biggest fan. If she hadn't made an appearance that day it would've certainly put a punctuation mark on whatever friendship remained. Her support kept a grin on my face as I paced the front of the classroom, enlightening my small audience of my calculated information and PowerPoint visuals. My mouth spilled knowledge as my eyes glanced to the back of the classroom to where she sat. I couldn't believe that just a few days prior, I had rejected her and left her kneeling in the rain, and there she was, caring enough to show her pretty face at my big presentation. Lydea's deed meant the world to me.

After my closing statement and model display, the students clapped with great noise. I gathered my items and joined her and my classmates in the back of the room.

"Jayden," Lydea corrected her posture, "I wanna let you know, the only reason I'm here is because you wanted me here from weeks ago."

"I'm still in shock that you came."

"Yeah, me too. I couldn't even look at you. Just being here hurts," she confessed, twirling her hair. "I don't remember half the things you said up there. Your major is like a different language to me. So, if you saw me in la la land, then I probably was."

The entire time I presented, I didn't care if she was listening to an iPod. Having her support felt good. It was comforting to see that she didn't turn her back on me, like I had done to her.

We parted minutes later, only to unexpectedly meet again on the second floor of the library. I saw Lydea studying by herself at an unfamiliar table, reviewing for her complicated final the next day. Despite her studying, I stood behind her and spoke in a gentle tone.

"Excuse me, is this seat taken?"

"No," she politely answered. "Take a seat."

"Thanks." I pulled out the chair and sat next to her, resting at the table, empty-handed. I sat there and watched her study, internally thanking the Lord that I was finished for the semester. *Don't stop learning, girl*, I said to myself. I loved her desire to be an A student. I wish my motivation to do well in school could've been sparked when I was her age. Too bad we can't retake life like we can classes, huh?

Lydea and I sat there, discussing the topic of her upcoming exam. Gradually, I brought up the incident that took place between her and Jason that past weekend. I didn't want to know the whole truth, but I hated to assume. In spite of the potential pain, I had to hear what happened from her mouth. I asked specific questions, and as I predicted, the words she spoke were the same ones that I didn't want to hear.

"Listen, Lyd, first off, I wanna apologize for not answering my phone Saturday night when you needed me. Can you put your pen down for a moment, please?" I asked, positioning my chair closer to hers. "I listened to all your voicemails, and read all your text messages. I just couldn't find a reason to answer my phone. I was still mad from what you told me in your room last Friday. But this whole week I've been itching to ask you this. What really happened that night? The night you were calling."

"Why do you wanna know now? It's not like you care," she replied, unmoved.

"I'll always care. Don't say that."

"Jayden, when I needed you, you weren't there for me. That's what hurts the most," she closed her binder.

"I know. I'm really, really sorry," I motioned. "But is it true that he raped you?" I whispered, trying to keep our conversation at the table.

"Yes," Lydea said, with her teeth clenched.

"How? Why? What kind of friend is he? How can you call him a friend?" I said, raising my hands with a lack of understanding.

"I don't know. I really don't know," she vented with her fists balled tight. "For starters, we waited for your butt to get outta work well past six and you never came out. So we left from Newport News and drove back to Norfolk. That's when the arguing began. He said the only way I was getting back to campus was if I walked. And then he kept yelling at me to get off the phone while I was calling you." She coughed to clear her dry throat. "I called you for hours, but I guess you had better things to do with your time. My classmates didn't pick up either. And to add to Jason's yelling at the apartment, he kept drinking. I hate when he drinks," she whispered in anger, looking around for anyone listening.

Out of nowhere, sitting at the table, the text message I thoughtlessly sent to Jason on Friday night shot across my mind. *She's all yours* rocked me with regret. I judged myself as being guilty for assisting in what happened. Lydea continued to express the tragedy that took place.

"It was going on midnight and Carla and Anthony still weren't home. Jason provoked me to fight him, but I resisted. I exerted all my strength to keep him off, but I eventually couldn't fight him off anymore. He's too strong, Jay. He's too damn strong. I simply covered my face while he held me down. I looked like a corpse," she went into further detail as my ears were tortured by her truth. "He held me down with pure rage. And I've never told anyone this but," she paused and took a deep breath, "this isn't the first time Jason's done something like this."

"What do you mean?"

"I mean, he did the same thing a year and a half ago. He held me down, saying that I owed it to him."

My temper increased. Jason never seemed to amaze me with his devilish actions. I knew I couldn't trust him.

"Yo, you want me to fight him? I'll do it," I said.

"No, Jayden, you don't have to fight him. I'm okay. Really. Fighting him won't change anything."

"No, really. I'll do it. But you know what's sad, Lyd?" I changed position. "You're right. Even if we threw hands, it'd all be in vain." I stared at her.

"Because you'd still go back to him, wouldn't you? This same criminal that you call a friend, you'd go back to. I can't wrap my mind around this."

"Can you keep this between me and you, please?"

"*No*. That's dumb! I can't be silent. Why haven't you told someone? Tell the police," I told her, pushing for justice.

"I ain't telling the police. You're the first person I've told and the last," she said, pointing dead at me, "which means that you can't tell anyone either. Traci doesn't even know."

"What? Yeah right," I softly shouted. "You'd be insane if you didn't speak up. I'll make the call for you if you're scared."

"I mean it. If you call the cops, I'll never talk to you again. Just act like you don't know anything, okay? I'll tell the police when and if I feel like it. Just leave it alone."

"Why do you call him your best friend after all he's done to you?" I asked, confounded.

"Well, he calls me his best friend, so I call him mine."

"No, no, no. Lydea, that's a terrible reason to claim *anyone* as a best friend," I corrected. "He doesn't deserve that title. I know you see that. You're so much smarter than this."

Once our conversation died down, I asked her to join me in between an aisle of bookshelves, away from the surrounding students. We stood alone. I looked in her eyes, gripping her shoulders, and hesitated to speak. "If I take you back, promise me that you will never jeopardize our relationship again. Aaaaand, *if* I take you back, then we gotta find a way for you to get back to New Jersey with your family. I can't be your man if you're living with that crazy dude," I said, still trying to understand why she would want to stay with him after all he had done.

"If you'll seriously take me back, then yes, I promise that I won't do anything stupid," Lydea said, convincingly. "And most importantly, I'll try my hardest to get back home."

"That's a promise?" I asked with a crooked smile as she nodded, taking me in her arms.

Later that night at my home, in bed with the lights off, a discomforting feeling arose in my stomach. My heart began to wrestle with my mind; my spirit argued with my soul; my pride belittled my humility, and my conscience mocked my ego. There was a battle royal going on inside of me and no one was winning. I repented to the Lord for not praying prior to taking Lydea back. Moments later, I was able to fall asleep, in peace.

Breakdown

What a roller coaster! I'm the stupid one though, right? I must've enjoyed the up-and-down relationship that I was in. I was physically off the ride and by my own free will decided to get back on it. I broke off my relationship for all the right reasons: my partner lacked all evidence of being loyal, my summer was going to be spent in Atlanta, and I was a fresh 22-two-year-old. I had enough justifications to settle in my singleness, but I wasn't completely liberated from the pull that kept me returning to my relationship. It was more than the Lord's commandment. It felt like a tugging at my soul. Who made the call to take her back? Was it my puzzled mind or my healing heart? I had no clue.

I realize now, it was my mercy and compassion for Lydea that brought her back into my arms that time around. I wanted her to be fully dependent on me for her needs, even if I couldn't supply them. I dreamt of being her knight in shining armor, but how dare I try to take care of her? I couldn't even sustain myself. I should've sought what the Lord wanted in prayer before I approached her table. Regardless of my choice, my word was my bond, and I was hers all over again.

~ Basking in the Sun ~

25

What an eventful week! Only a week like this could end with an all-day affair, right? Friday was the day before housing kicked everyone off campus and Lydea insisted that I help her. My excuses fell short, so there I stood, surrounded by her possessions. I scanned her room and noticed clothes were everywhere. I thought to myself, *How can one girl own all this stuff?* There were shirts, dress pants, skirts, jeans, jean jackets, leather jackets, sweatshirts, sweaters, socks, undergarments, and shoes on top of shoes that still needed to be boxed. I even spotted a few tagged outfits splayed across the bed. It was insane! She was a walking department store. It was definitely too much for the average guy to appreciate.

"I can't believe all these clothes are yours," I told her, sitting on her roommate's bed, who was never there.

"Yeah, things add up over time," Lydea replied, contending with the volume of the VH1 special. "Good thing it's my last semester doing this dormitory thing."

"Really?" I said turning down the television. "That's good to hear. Hopefully you'll get some more closet space 'cause this is ridiculous."

After packing we heaved several boxes into my illegally parked car. Vehicles large and small were scattered all over campus. I rushed her as we worked, beading with sweat on the hottest day of spring. The moment my Honda was securely packed to the windows, the two of us crammed in and took the short eight-mile drive to Jason's spot, where she'd be staying. I stumbled up the metal apartment stairs with my hands full and lightly knocked, pushing the cracked door open. At that hour, only Jason's roommates, Anthony and Carla, were there.

"Yo, yo," I greeted, stepping into the living room.

"Hey, Jay," Carla responded, sitting on her dining room chairs with Anthony, drinking beer and playing Xbox 360 on their small TV. "Lydea's stuff is going in that back room on the right. There should be enough space next to the bed for it all. I wish we had a couch for her to sleep on, you know?"

"Who you telling? I'll give my leg for one right now."

"She'll be aight. She knows what she's doing," Carla sarcastically announced, as Lydea followed several steps behind me into the room, saying nothing to her housemates.

The madness that had taken place the weekend before troubled my thoughts. Despite the discomfort, I continued to work until my car was bare. We made a second exhausting trip from campus back to the apartment. The physical strain of lifting plus the sun's sizzling heat had us depleted. I knew that she had no one else to assist her, so I hoped that my good deed was making up for my previous absence.

After the last load was brought in, I sprawled across Jason's bed, exhausted. "So, Jay, what are we gonna do after we rest?" Lydea asked. "We can't sit around this apartment all day."

"Why are you even *thinking* about doing something else right now?" I grunted, sliding off the bed and on to the floor. "That proves you didn't work hard enough, you lazy bum. Give me thirty minutes. Think of something while I sleep."

"You hear that?" she said looking attentive. "I think I hear the beach calling my name."

"Naaah, nah. Are you for real?" I flailed my arms. "C'mon, Lyd, give my car a break. Let's go to the campus pool or something."

"The campus pool? Yeah right. You won't find me in that pool. Plus, we haven't been to the beach since we've been a couple. There's a towel in your trunk. C'mon, it will be fun. I promise," she assured, sitting on the floor next to me. "This way I can wear my new lime green bathing suit that I bought a few weeks ago. I can't wait to put it on."

Lydea continued to talk as I sat with my back against the bed and dozed off. Exactly 30 minutes later, I felt gentle taps on the bridge of my nose.

"Wake up, sleepy head," her sweet accent whispered.

"Whaaat?" I groaned, shifting my shoulders.

"Wake up, we need to get going. It's almost three o'clock. Get up, Jay. I have a surprise for you."

"I don't wanna wake up," I groaned some more.

"Okay, fine. You don't wanna wake up, then I got something that will wake you up. Look at my bathing suit. Tell me if you like it," she teased.

I slowly turned my head in her direction and cracked one eye open to see what she was taking about. "Oh nah!" I jumped wide-awake. "I *know* you ain't wearing that. You better have a turtleneck to put on over that, girl. I ain't playin'."

"Fine." Lydea laughed. "I knew that would wake you up. I have a top and bottom for it. Don't worry. I'll be covered."

Soon after gaining strength, the two of us hopped in my car and drove east on the interstate towards the oceanfront with the intent of getting nothing more than our feet wet. Cruising along, I had my sunroof back, my windows down and my music up. "Who sings this song?" she asked while the humid breeze blew through her hair. "I like it."

"Girl, this is Frankie Beverly and Maze!"

"What's the name of it? Turn it up."

"Yeah! This is 'Joy and Pain', Lyd. It's a classic."

Swaying to the throwback, we missed the message behind the lyrics. It pinpointed our relationship and we didn't even realize it.

Once we arrived on the beach, we snapped pictures in our beach attire. "Say cheese," I said, kicking sand her way as she posed for the shot. Like youngsters at a playground, she chased me for the camera. I laughed and gave up the chase, falling onto the beach towel with her. Our day was going great just as she promised.

By late evening, the transition had started and a separate crowd had arrived. The club folks were populating the streets. We eventually got dressed and left Virginia Beach to the night owls. Approaching my Accord, Lydea spoke up, "Okay, I've been thinking. Since we're back together, I have to do what's right." With quickness, she snatched the keys straight from my hand and skipped to my driver's side. My feet shuffled close behind her as I tickled her ribs. She spun around to face me, dangling my bulky keys near my eyes. I attempted to grab them, but she bounced them around my grasp, filled with amusement. "Not so fast, Mr. Man. Due to your birthday being this past Monday, I'm obligated to still get you something. You'll except a few late birthday gifts, won't you?" She grinned showing off the depth of her left dimple.

"Yes, baby girl," I answered.

"Good," she said, sliding my keys back into my hand, and firmly pressing her lips against mine for a sweet kiss. Our time as a couple felt refreshing again, almost like we had never broken up. I cranked up my car, feeling alive, and sped off to the Wal-Mart back in Norfolk.

My girl shopped as I watched her from a distance. She didn't care if I saw the gifts she bought me. I knew her intent was to make them unique and special, and indeed they were. The final item was a small chocolate cake, which we both selected together. Even though her gifts were late, they actually meant more to me than those that I received on the day of my birthday.

"Thanks, babe," I said with a rocking squeeze in front of the cashier.

"Is all of this for you?" the young brunette asked.

"Yeah," I said, holding Lydea. "I gotta good lady."

"I'd say," the girl agreed. "You make me want to buy *my* boyfriend a few things," she directed at my girl.

"Do it." Lydea giggled. "He would enjoy that."

"I will." She smiled, handing us our bags. "Thanks. Enjoy your night."

We left with my random gifts and drove off into the night, feeling like we had all the time in the world.

"Hey, there's a secret spot downtown that I've been wanting to show you for some time," I mentioned while driving directionless. After several U-turns, I parked along this open townhouse community, right where I wanted us to be. Lydea stepped out, holding the cake and plasticware, as we walked our way towards the large pond that was encircled by a freshly paved sidewalk, young trees, bright street lamps, and new wooden benches. The two of us relaxed in the warm breeze of May, conversing, being joined again. For hours, we chatted about our past, present, and future. We grazed the topic of the approaching summer, as well as when and how she was going to get a job. There were plenty of questions and not enough answers. We shared the chocolate cake, passing forkfuls into each other's mouth like a couple in love should.

"All right, Lyd, I know we spoke about this several times already, but tell me again how you plan on breaking free from Jason?" I asked, licking my fork clean. "Time to start being independent, girl."

"I know. I know. You sound like my father. It's harder than you think. Jason is always throwing himself at me. 'Let me buy you this. Let me take you there.' He's always giving me something. How can I turn him down?" she wondered, shoving another slice my way.

"By sayin' no!" I blurted with my mouth full. "Check this out, once you get to New Jersey and start working, you can rely on yourself and not worry about his gifts anymore. Doesn't your pops still have your Nissan?"

"Yeah, it's in Camden."

"Well, okay then. There you go. What's the problem?"

"He plans on selling it. The car note is too high."

"Tell him not to. Tell him that you'll drive it to work and help pay it off."

Lydea shrugged. "School should be my only focus. I really don't want to work, Jayden. It'll just make me mad."

"Going to work will not make you mad. That's nonsense. A good job is only gonna build your character. Shoot, a *bad* job will build your character—what am I talkin' about?" I caught myself. "Don't worry about what kind of job it is, just try to get one. And when you do, remember that *you* manage your money. After you give a tenth to the Lord, the amount you spend and save is all up to you. A job will be great for you this summer."

"I don't know," Lydea replied, unsure.

"Really. It'll keep you busy. Plus, you can meet some new girlfriends. And we both know that you could use some of them."

"Whatever, boy," she said, crossing her legs.

"Can you at least try to be productive this summer?" I requested. "Will you do that for me?"

"I guess," she said grinning, cutting into the last slice to share with me. "I guess I can do that for you, Jay."

A lengthy day like this one created a lot of good emotions within me. I didn't want my feelings to get carried away again, so I continued to guard my heart. By 1 a.m., I returned Lydea to her summer residence and escorted her to the door. We exchanged our first genuine kiss since our breakup, and it felt great.

Breakdown

I can't explain it. Does love have an explanation? Why did I feel such an emotional tug towards Lydea? How could I love this girl to the point that I was able to see past her flaws and shortcomings? Why was I so fast to forgive her after all the tears I had cried? Did I really love Lydea? Does true love keep a record of wrongs? I guess not. I guess you can consider me a sucker for love. A man of second chance. And third chance. And fourth chance, and so on.

In Matthew 18:21–22, Jesus' disciple, Peter, asked him if seven times were sufficient enough to forgive someone that offended him. Jesus answered, *"I say not unto you seven times, but seventy times seven."*

Whoa! In the Lord's eyes there seemed to be no end to forgiving someone and taking them back. I reminded myself of what God had commanded of me. There were even moments when I prided myself in being the chosen one to save Lydea, and not Jesus. But the Holy Spirit never asked me to bring her to salvation. All my Savior wanted me to do was introduce Lydea to him, help build her character, and be Christ-like while doing it. It's a shame that I was miles away from doing either one. Basking in the sun stole my dependency from the Lord. The good times became a distraction. This was probably why God didn't hold back my upcoming rain.

~ Broken Promises ~

26

If anyone asked me back then how my love life was, I couldn't answer them. I was confused and didn't know what to think. I didn't need a girlfriend during college, but I wanted one. No matter how many obstacles came my way, I still wanted Lydea. Only through God's grace was I able to find enough love and kindness deep inside of me to cope with Jason's involvement. I had barely enough love inside of me to share with Lydea so she could feel loved.

This relationship of ours is destined to be, I told myself. My family was whole and hers was fractured. My future looked bright and hers just needed clouds removed. She was book-smart and I was creative. I knew the Lord and she needed to hear his voice. I believed Lydea was the color in my painting, but was this love?

One day, after hearing a message from Bishop T. D. Jakes, a powerful man of God, I changed my perspective on this entire love thing. He gave a sermon televised on the Trinity Broadcasting Network (TBN) that opened my eyes. "Only in God's math can one plus one equal one," Jakes said with wisdom. "We shouldn't want someone to complete us or to become our better half, but instead we should want to be whole already. So once you're whole and your partner is whole, then together you can *be* whole, lacking nothing."

Yes! Completion. Wholeness. This was something neither Lydea nor I had. Glancing into our relational rearview mirror, I saw the mountains that we had climbed. I often said with optimism, "We can do this!" But my lingering insecurities disabled all hope for completion.

To better understand how I felt, listen to the song by the underground R&B artist, Van Hunt, entitled "Down Here in Hell (With You)". The song title alone speaks volumes to me. I often compared our struggling relationship with getting out of hell. I felt as if the exit was floored with boiling quicksand and no matter how hard I tried to flee, I was sucked right back in. I comforted myself by thinking, *As long as the both of us are in hell together, I'll never be alone.* But what an ignorant belief that was. For I know the reality of hell is an unquenchable fire, a terrible place without an exit. However I had actually saved myself from the relationship four times already, escaping from the mental state of hell, yet still running back to rescue her. Did I *really* want to go back though? The lyrics to this song became so real to me because I've been there. I kept this track on repeat for days.

The first weekend Lydea and Jason stayed together was unbearable. So many questions shot off the walls of my mind. *How am I supposed to deal with this?* I wondered, filled with assumptions. The inquiry I dealt with didn't want to hear an answer, but my accountability to her forced me to open my mouth.

"Soooo, you wanna tell me where you slept last night?" I unwillingly poked over the phone.

"Does it matter?" she said, questioning my question.

"Listen, I already know that your sleeping conditions are ugly. Boxes and bags were spread all over his bedroom floor days ago, so I'm just curious as to where—"

"If you must know, I slept in his bed last night, okay?"

"Did Jason sleep in the bed too?" I asked.

"Unfortunately, yes," she mumbled.

Yep, there it was, the truth and a broken promise. My assumptions were right. What was I to think? What could I do? How much faith should I have in this girl? I could barely trust her and we know that my trust for him was definitely non-existent. That weekend, I slept very little. I struggled to endure her situation. The Sunday after my work shift, I listened to a message on my phone of Lydea shouting and begging me to come get her. Without delaying, I made my way to their complex in Norfolk. I had to prove myself reliable. I dialed her number while I drove, hoping she would pick up.

"Hello?" she answered after the first ring.

"Yo, Lyd, what's up? You good?" I said, concerned.

"I am now. Are you still coming?" she said with desperation, anticipating my arrival. "Jayden, please say yes."

"Yeah, yeah. I'm passing Hampton University now. What was wrong earlier? You sounded upset."

"It's a long story. Jason punched a few holes in the wall, that's all. I'll tell you more when you get here, okay? Just hurry, please."

I was tired and smelled like a yard dog, but my lady needed me. I pulled into the complex and there she was, sitting on the stoop. She jumped to her feet once she recognized my car and ran up to greet me. Our tight embrace was extensive. She was so happy to see me. "Let's walk," I told her.

We paced the area until it became dangerously late. "Lyd, you gotta leave this place before something bad happens," I implored.

"Where am I gonna go?" she replied. "You know my uncle sold his house. And the last time I spoke with my father, he kept complaining about his headaches; talking about he didn't want to hear about my problems. Him and his new wife have an extra room and I can't even stay there."

"See, that right there is upsetting," I said.

"Exactly," she agreed. "My dad is a jerk."

Instantly, her father went from being a civilized man in my eyes to a shameful one. He wasn't even trying to help.

"All I know is—you can't stay here with Jason. You just can't," I emphasized, standing in a parking space next to a dirty pickup truck. "We're not talking a weekend or even a few short weeks. You're looking at an entire summer of holes in the walls. You have to find somewhere else to stay! This ain't your home."

"Where? With who?" she shouted. "Jayden, I have nowhere else to go. My own father doesn't want me around! What can I do? I have no job. I have no car. Jason is being nice enough to give me a place. He doesn't have to let me stay here, you know?"

"Oh please! You said this was Carla's spot. That dude's renting a room. This ain't his apartment," I argued under the flickering streetlight.

"Whatever." She sucked her teeth. "Just know, deep down inside of me, I don't want to be here either." She walked away. "I have no other choice, Jay."

"Yes, you do," I encouraged her. "Keep pushing."

With both hands in the air, she motioned a sign of surrender up to God, releasing a blast of rage into the starless sky. "Lord! If my mom was still alive, I wouldn't have this problem. Jesus, I know you hear me!"

Breakdown

Was there really no way out for my girl? Every secondary option I suggested, she responded with a rationale not to leave. Traci, Lydea's best friend, offered her a room in Delaware with her family, but at the last moment, Traci decided to remain at her university for summer school. Lydea's older cousin, Malix, in Connecticut, opened a door of opportunity for her to stay and be employed at the lodging company that he owned. I knew surely this was her ticket! Unfortunately, he reneged on his offer. There was a small probability that she could get a cheap apartment in Norfolk or Chesapeake while she worked, but how could she work without transportation? The city bus was an option; still, nothing was written in stone. In Lydea's unspoken words, all of her belongings looked quite comfortable on Jason's bedroom floor.

What kind of relationship did I get myself into? I frequently wondered. Was this my reality or was I living an endless nightmare? It felt like the modern day version of *The Never Ending Story,* without all the enchantment, of course. This wasn't what I had signed up for. This wasn't what she had promised me.

~ Circles and Triangles ~

27

The days rolled into weeks, and my thoughts floated along. I swam in a pool of assumptions. My pessimistic thinking created terrible suspicion that lead to unnecessary judgments. I reminded myself that Lydea's situation was out of my control. I knelt down along my bedside in prayer, asking the Lord to relieve us of our burdens. When I prayed, I could no longer worry. I had to have faith that God could and would change Lydea's circumstance. The moment I lifted it up to God, the battle wasn't ours anymore. I begged him for his amazing grace, hoping that he would give us a blessing that we didn't deserve. I also reminded him of his everlasting mercy so he would withhold the consequences that we *did* deserve. In order for her to get out of this deep, dark hole, much grace was needed.

Throughout the weekdays, while everyone was at work, Lydea was left alone at the apartment. When Carla and Anthony had days off, they usually occupied the living room as my lady settled in the privacy of Jason's room, waiting for him to return from his job.

"Jayden, I'm not here to make friends, okay?" she told me, as I stood outside of the pet store on my 30 minute lunch break. "Except for the seldom hellos and good-byes, I have nothing to say to them. I seclude myself so I can stay out of their business. They gossip too much over here. I know they talk about me. Why should I speak any more than what I do?"

"Because, they're letting you stay there. Don't be an outcast, Lyd," I told her, watching a teenage couple pass me by, laughing and fumbling two Chocolate Labrador puppies. "Break all that hostility. At least *try* to be friends with them. Being an introvert ain't gonna make things any better," I added, playing coach.

"I'm not here to make friends," she repeated, inflexible. "There's too much tension in this place. I feel it."

"Well, do something about it then. Break the tension."

After that conversation, days went by without hearing from her. Until one late evening, I received a call from an unavailable number. I answered it, clueless as to who it was.

"Hello?"

"Hey, it's me. I'm calling you from a payphone," Lydea said. "I don't want to be the bearer of bad news, but I'm letting you know that Jason threw the cell phone across the room two nights ago and destroyed it."

"He broke his own phone? He did it on purpose, huh?"

"Yeah, I think so. He's been checking our minutes again. Looks like I'll have to use 7-Eleven's phone for now."

"Well, that certainly ain't good news. That's for sure."

"I know. What can I say? If you'd like, I can get him to walk me here every night so I can call you," she offered. "It would give me a reason to leave the apartment at least. How does that sound?"

"If that's our only option, I'll take what I can get. Do you think he'll walk with you every night though?"

"Yeah, I'll make him walk or drive. Either one he'll do," she said with assurance. "But let me go. He's giving me a look. Talk to you tomorrow, Jay. I love you."

"I love you too, babe."

I couldn't believe it. I was actually in a love triangle! I was strapped down onto this transparent, three corner, geometrical shape with my girlfriend and an unwanted third party. *Great,* I thought, *so now what?* How could I reach her when I was available? When Lydea and I did speak via payphone, it was brief and to the point, verbally planning the days ahead. Thanks to Jason, this horrible friend of hers destroying his phone, he was now able to take advantage of long walks with Lydea just so we could speak for two brief minutes. If one evening went by and a call wasn't made from her end, I took it as a sign and my negative assumptions started to get the best of me again. So on that particular evening when my cell phone didn't ring, I examined my heart. In my free time, I expressed myself through the lead of a pencil and scribbled the following:

If I had listened to my heart a long time ago, I wouldn't be in this situation. My girlfriend is staying with a friend that likes her, and he acts like a mental patient. He buys her things and gives her what she needs. Her family is unstable; they can't give her what she needs. I come into the picture to give her what she really needs. All I get in return is a heart that starts to bleed. Emotionally, I'm so tired. Why go any further? This dude intimidates her. He's actually thought of murder. They've never been a couple, but he claims to love her just the same. The only attachment that she has to him is the money that he spends. And she says he's just a friend. Never that. My heart was right to leave from the very beginning. But it's like I prayed, and prayed, and God gave me a crooked thumbs up. The nice guy in me was hoping for lots of good luck. Now I'm in a love triangle and I hope I'm not stuck. Either I go or he goes, I'm not going to tug. Who do you love? Are you for sure? It's all or nothing. I'm closing my door. But I won't lock it, because what was meant to be will be, and if the man in your life wasn't meant to be me, then I'll understand and walk away freely.

Breakdown

It's an awful experience for a man to deal with another man spending time with the lady who he cares so deeply for. My heart provoked me with much grief, *If you don't hear from Lydea, then she probably doesn't want to talk to you,* it would say. *She has Jason, remember?* My mind continued to reason with my heart. Those two inner parts of me were always bumping heads. Jason didn't need to spend any more time with her than what came naturally; however, I silently supported him footing it with her during the late evening hours so I could hear her voice. Yet, corrupted loyalty was all I saw. Call it envy, insecurity, or a lack of faith all you want to, but no man in his right mental state would've tried to walk in my shoes. The shoes I wore during this season of my life hurt my feet too much to tread; still I endured, in spite of the pain.

~ Smiles and Sins ~

28

The month of May was one to remember. When I wasn't with my girlfriend, I spent my time working behind the register, daydreaming and eagerly awaiting my upcoming summer in Atlanta. My future was looking good, but my present was a different story.

On a particularly gray and dreary afternoon, away from the pet store, I was with Lydea on the other side of the peninsula. To pass the time, we watched a silly comedy while eating hot buttered popcorn in the living room by ourselves. Chuckling throughout the simple movie didn't remove the awkward feeling of Carla's messy place and Jason's punched holes in the wall. After the movie, Lydea led me to the bedroom to grab a magazine article. I glanced at the bed and noticed it was made up with her sheets, blankets, and colorful pillows. In utter shock, I yelled, "What's this?"

"What's what?" she said, looking at my facial expression. "The bed? What's wrong with the bed?"

"Oh c'mon, Lydea! Do you have to get *this* comfortable? Why are you killing his room with all your stuff?" I said, standing at the doorway, refusing to walk in.

"Jayden, please. I know where my sheets have been. Jason, on the other hand, only God knows."

"I thought we agreed that when the floor was less cluttered you'd sleep there."

She leaned over the bed to grab the magazine, causing my eyes to sweat. "Well…I mean…okay, fine, that was our agreement, but look at the floor. I slept down there *one* night and got bit three times. Look at these marks on my calf," she said, rolling up her left Capri pant leg. "Plus, Jason won't let me sleep down there. He says there's enough space in the bed for the both of us."

"I don't care what he said. We had an agreement. Didn't you distinctly tell me a few weeks ago that you *promise* to not do anything stupid? What do you think you're doing?"

"But…"

"No, no." I pumped my finger. "You see how fast promises get broken. This is why I don't make promises. This right here," I slammed the magazine back onto the bed, "is exactly why I, Jayden Rockaway, do not make promises."

"I'm sorry for breaking my promise, but throw me a frickin' bone here. I'm in the ghetto! Can I at least sleep in a bed while I'm here?"

"No!" I shouted with a grin. "The ghetto bugs like your legs, so give them what they want. And I'm your boyfriend so give me what I want too."

Moments settled. "I know what you want." She batted her eyes, slowly revealing her bra strap.

"You better stop." I backed up. "You know we shouldn't—"

"I'll give you what you want, Papi," Lydea said, pulling me towards the bed. "Right now."

Within moments, we found something to do. No fear at all. If all else failed, there was always that one thing. Afterwards, we left the apartment and drove to our favorite Chinese restaurant, insensitive to our sin.

Two days later I was given another day off from work, so Lydea and I met up once again. Our plans were to either go to Busch Gardens in Williamsburg, the Norfolk Zoo, or take a trip to Mt. Trashmore, a well-known park in Virginia Beach. The zoo was in our plans from several months prior, but we never made it there. Mt. Trashmore got our vote for the day, and Virginia's weather couldn't have been more perfect. This was the kind of day that allowed us to bask in the sun without a worry of sunburn. We swung through a nearby grocery store and bought random picnic items to enjoy at the peak of the 60-foot, grass covered mountain. We spread out in the sod-like grass and enjoyed our meals in the pleasant heat, experiencing a peaceful moment in time.

"Babe, I don't know what it is about us, but we have one of the craziest relationships ever made!" I bragged.

"You think so? Why's that?"

"I'll tell you why. Who else do you know has broken up as many times as we have and still have things to laugh about? We could easily write a book about our relationship. It'd probably make a good movie too, you think?"

"A book? A movie? You've lost your mind, boy. All that we've been through is not book or movie material. Yes, we've had our share of drama, but c'mon."

"I'm serious. The storyline would be great."

"Lemme guess," she said, grabbing my plastic knife to cut into her sandwich. "You'd play the protagonist, Jason would be the antagonist, and I'd be lady y'all fight over."

"Exactly! Now you're seeing through my eyes!" I exclaimed.

"Not gonna happen, playa." Lydea shook her head, shooting down my hopes. "Forget about it."

After finishing our lunch, the gnats soon destroyed our nirvana. We gathered our trash and stumbled down the hill, holding hands, and laughing hysterically. Once we made it to flat ground, we walked the paved track, understanding that our days were accounted for.

"Jayden, I don't want you to leave next week," my girl said. "I can't be left with Jason knowing you're not around. Do you really have to go to Georgia again this summer?"

"No. I don't *have* to go. I *need* to go," I said. "Don't you want me to better myself?"

"Yeah, of course I do. But why can't you better yourself here? I'm sure there are plenty of internships in Newport News."

"It won't be the same," I told her, squeezing our grip. "That's exactly why my city's nickname is 'Badnews'. Kinda speaks for itself, huh? Anyways, how about this, how about if you come to Atlanta next month and pay me a visit?" I asked in full stride. "Does that sound good?"

"Yeah, we'll see. That's not a bad idea to tell you the truth. I'll go if you buy the ticket."

We went back and forth, thinking up ideas. However, time would be the ultimate storyteller of what the future had in store. Little did I know what my night had in store.

I eventually parked my car back at the apartment complex as an unknown number appeared on my phone. "Who's this?" I wondered out loud, showing Lydea the number.

"Oh, that's Jason's number. He had an old phone reactivated today."

"Hello?"

"Ayo, is Lyd around?" Jason inquired, modestly.

I turned the music low and passed her my phone. "It's for you," I said in a bass tone.

"Hello?" Lydea said, putting him on speakerphone.

"Yo, what's crackin'? I'm not interrupting am I?" he asked, as I listened in.

"No. We're not doing anything. Why? What's up?"

"Oh, nothin' much. Just wanted to let you know that I'll be at my sister's crib for the night. She needs my help with a lot of things, so if your boy wants to hang around, he can. It's aight with me."

"Really? Okay. Well, I'll see what he wants to do. Thanks for the offer, I guess. Um, I'll see you tomorrow?"

"Yeah, I'll be around after work. Aight? But I'll let you go."

"Okay, Jas. Thanks. Bye." She hung up and handed me back my phone. "Did you hear him?"

I remained quiet, questioning his motives. I sat still, wondering why he was allowing me stay. "I'm not sure," I said confused.

"Come," she insisted, tugging on my wrist. We got out of the car, and I followed her into the apartment like an ox to the slaughterhouse. Anthony and Carla watched TV in the living room on their box-like dining chairs, as my eyes were once again drawn to the punched holes in the wall. Lydea interrupted my trance. "Stop looking at those," she said, pulling me away.

"I think you should stay a lil' longer and keep me company," she persuaded by the hallway coat closet. "Whatcha say?"

I looked into her seductive eyes and began to stutter. "But first—" she covered my mouth with her hand, "take a shower. The weather got you smelling like some old man's feet. I'll get you a towel."

"Yeah, good lookin' out, stinky." I twisted my lips. "I hope you do the same. And why do you know what old men's feet smell like?"

"Whatever." She giggled. "My sweat smells a lot better than yours right now. Don't even go there."

By this time, it was fairly late, pushing 11 p.m.. I followed her advice and took a shower. Once I came out, she did the same and returned to the bedroom clothed in a short pastel nightgown. The lust in me yelled out, *Here we go again!* I couldn't believe my situation. I rested next to Lydea, fighting the idea that Jason slept in the same bed every night. If the enticement was that strong for me and she was my girl, I couldn't imagine what traveled through his mind.

The two of us stretched out our legs with the television producing the only light in the room. The moment she cut it off, her soft fingers filled the grooves of mine. Positioned near the edge of the bed, I held her hand, still fighting the feeling. Slowly but surely, we inched closer until our bodies touched from lips to toes. Clothing was replaced with smooth skin. Oh, the pleasure of sin is a feeling that many could describe. Our hearts raced in the midst of our actions. I moved to the rhythm of the music that we made. When all had calmed down, we held one another and dozed off in each other's arms until the alarm clock broke our sleep at 5:10 a.m.

We both knew I couldn't risk staying the whole night. I needed my car to be in the driveway before my mother and father left for work in the morning. I quickly got dressed and gathered my loose articles. I kissed Lydea good-bye and left the apartment with a thin layer of guilt covering my thoughts. I sped home, parked behind my brother's car, and crept up the house stairs. I heard my sister's radio going off behind her closed room door for her to arise for school. No one knew where I had been or what I had just done. I was safe. No one knew—but God.

Breakdown

So many nights of rebellion, I can't recall them all. When do our sinful ways cease? This particular sin has made many of us climb out of second-story windows, hide in bedroom closets, roll underneath beds, and lie to parents, all because we're afraid of getting caught. This blows my mind. If we don't want to get caught, then why do we still do it? The thrill of *not* getting caught is a comedy all in itself. I've heard classic stories throughout my college years of others *almost* getting caught doing wicked acts. As funny as it may seem at the time, there is nothing funny about begging for forgiveness and paying the consequences for our wrongs.

So what if Jason didn't catch me or my parents didn't know? I wasn't thinking about Lydea's father finding out what I was doing with his daughter. My fear wasn't in them knowing what I was doing behind closed doors. And as shameful as this is to admit as a Christian, my fear wasn't in God knowing either. But he sees everything! Good and evil. Who should I fear more, man or God? The cops or the King? My parents or Jesus? I knew who to fear more, as I'm sure most of us do, so then why didn't I flee in my conviction? In response to satisfying my flesh with sex, my Savior was not pleased with me, and I knew it.

~ More Sins and More Smiles ~

29

Still in much doubt concerning my relationship, the weekend before my departure, I shared my dilemma with the fellas during a game of spades, at Cassell's mama's house.

"Ayo, man. I need y'all's opinion on something," I spoke up, as we sat around the dining table. "What should I do with my girl this summer? I'm gonna be gone for like two, three months."

"Stay with her," one of them shouted from the kitchen.

"*I think you betta let it go*," Cassell sang like Teddy Pendergrass, bringing everyone to laughter.

"I say you break up with her, yo," another voiced. "Long distance relationships never work out."

I heard several responses. The majority agreed that I should simply move on, but I continued to argue my point. "Yeah, that's easy for y'all to say," I uttered, spinning the big joker in the center of the table. "I got feelings for this girl, man. I can't walk away like that. Have you seen my girl? She's *bad*."

"Feelings?" Cassell blurted. "Are we talkin' about feelings in a room full of men? Jay, the dude your girl's staying with got feelings!" he said, bringing everyone to an uproar. "Yo, I hate to tell you this, bruh, but *it looks like another love T. K. O.!*"

"Whatever, yo," I said under my breath as they laughed away. "Whatever. Whose turn is it?"

My friends were no help. Not one of them could sympathize with me. My situation couldn't be understood. Lydea and I spoke that Sunday after church and I continued to push New Jersey as her destination for the summer.

"Lyd, you can do this," I assured, later that night over the phone. "I'll get you there if you need me to."

"*You?* I won't hold my breath on that one."

"Why's that? I'll do it. It's a small sacrifice. I know."

"You're leaving in a few days, Jay. Really, it's okay."

"No, it's not okay," I opposed. "If we're staying together, you ain't living with your boy. We already talked about this."

"I know. My Uncle Carlos reminded me about this extended stay motel outside the city the other day," she said, "but it's mostly an all men's spot. *Old* men, from what I remember. I refuse to stay out there."

"Well, I don't blame you on that one. Bad suggestion," I said, switching my cell phone from one ear to the other. "Oh, by the way, Tuesday is our last day to chill."

"Why? I thought you weren't leaving until Thursday."

"Yeah, that's what I said, but I gotta work all day Monday and early Wednesday. Plus Wednesday's my sister's birthday. We're supposed to take her out that evening."

"I thought we were gonna spend more time than that," Lydea griped over the speakerphone. "You promised."

"Hey, hey, hey, I didn't promise that. I said, I'd see what I could do. So...I'm gonna see what I can do."

By Tuesday, I was in Norfolk at the strike of noon. It was a sorrowful day for the both of us, but we couldn't spend it disheartened. The climate was unseasonably hot, and we both dressed accordingly. Our dark shades and vacation-like attire allowed us to ride with liberation. For most of the afternoon we drove around, shopping and eating. The idea of scarfing down a delicious cookies and cream waffle cone from Bruster's began as a thought and then became reality. I couldn't believe this was our last day together. We ended our final day by replaying memories of our relationship, until Graham's phone call interrupted us as we pulled back into the complex.

"Jay-Money, what's good for the night, kid?"

"It's whatever, man. Me and Lyd are just getting back to Carla's crib. Where you at?"

"I'm in their living room right now. I was about to leave. Gimme a second."

My lady stepped out the car with a strange look on her face. Within an instant, Graham met us in the parking lot.

"Yo, what's poppin'?" I greeted, dapping him up.

"Chillin', man," he said, stretching his arms out to hug my girl. "I'm 'bouta meet a few college friends at Roger Brown's sports bar if y'all tryin' to roll?"

Lydea was already awaiting my question. I turned to ask, but before I even opened my mouth, she sucked her teeth with an attitude. "You can go. I don't care."

Now, "I don't care" coming from her had two meanings: *If you go, then you're gonna regret it,* and *I really don't care.* It took me months to differentiate the two. So I took her words literally and the moment I agreed to leave with Graham, Lydea's temper was immediately sparked. She pushed her waffle cone into my hands and stormed away.

"Dang, you said you didn't care. What's all this?" I asked baffled, trailing behind her towards the apartment. Without a second thought, I turned back to Graham. "Yo, man, ol' girl's trippin'. We made plans to chill tonight. Just us two. You know how it is."

"Yeah, I guess," he shrugged. "She *said* she didn't care. But you know her better than me."

"Nah, I'm *still* getting to know the girl," I said, giving him a hard pound. "When Lyd says, 'I don't care,' the meaning is all in her body language. That doesn't confuse me anymore. But yo, be good tonight, man," I said, backpedaling. "I got some business to take care of. Enjoy your summer, G. I'll holla."

Lydea stood on the stoop with her arms folded, waiting for my return. While Graham drove off, my phone rang. I thought it was him.

"What up, son?" I answered.

"Yo, Jay. This is Jason. Is Lyd around?" I grunted and quickly hit the speaker button.

"Here."

She snatched the phone from my hand, still upset. "Hey Jas," she said turning her backside to me.

"Hey, you good?" he questioned.

"Yeah, I could be worse. I'm outside of your place."

"Oh, that's cool. Don't mind me then. I just wanted to give you a heads up. I'll be in Chesapeake again tonight helping my sis, so the room's all yours if you want it."

"Again?" she speculated. "Why are you so giving?"

"Whatever, girl. *Mi casa es su casa*."

"Yeah. Well, thanks, I guess. See you tomorrow."

"Aight," Jason said through the phone. "Gone."

Wow, a second chance to repeat a sinful act. The devil was once again the DJ as temptation and opportunity danced themselves to the beat. I avoided the topic for a while, but sure enough, I got lured on to the dance floor by temptation. Lydea and I drove to the 7-Eleven so I could be responsible for my soon-to-be actions. She sat reserved in the passenger seat, still venting over my quick response to leave with Graham. But riding back to the apartment, my silly ways uplifted her mood. Even in Jason's room, I remained lighthearted. As our final hours approached, we knew how the night was going to conclude.

We stayed on opposite ends of the bed, writing our farewell cards to each other, allowing the time to tick away. Our feelings made it easy to smother the cards with emotive phrases. Once our last punctuation mark was placed, we sealed the cards shut, put them in our farewell gift bags and exchanged them. Her bag contained a three-part poem and her favorite chocolates. Within my bag was a picture of us in a frame. Tears built up in her eyes as we stared at each other. At the appointed time, the lamp was cut off and an old Eric Benet CD brought a sensual vibe to the room. Our cards were pushed aside, making space for our outstretched bodies. A lustful passion lingered like mist around the bed. I realized exactly what I was getting myself into. The urge to touch her lips, which seemed to drip with honey, was overwhelming. Her strawberries and champagne scented lotion melted my righteousness. She sat up to undress and her shadow projected against the wall from the streetlight outside of the sheer-curtained window. The lust in me was building fast. It was an uncontrollable lust that I called love. We boasted our thoughts softly into each other's ear. If this was how "love" felt outside of marriage, I could only imagine what the night of an untainted honeymoon would feel like.

We continued with an endless stamina, wanting the moment to last forever. Our kisses never went dry. Oh, how could this be wrong when it felt so right? For the first time in our relationship, my mind and flesh yearned for the same thing. Lydea brought chemistry to the room that I didn't know she possessed. Her body heat felt like a nearby fireplace. She crept near my earlobe and gently breathed, "Jayden, I'm in love with you." Her words brought the hair on my neck to a standstill. She then proceeded in Spanish.

We went back and forth, love wrestling. I held her tight in my arms, not letting her go until the alarm clock awoke us at 4 a.m. Unlike last time, I didn't want to leave. Despite sleeping in the devil's bed, I forced myself to go.

"I'm gonna miss you, baby," I said lowly, standing next to the bed, straightening my light blue Polo shirt.

"I'm going to miss you more," Lydea stated with a clear and sad voice, still curled up under the covers. "I can't sleep. I've been awake this whole time."

"Really?" I asked.

"Yeah. My thoughts won't let me rest."

"Your thoughts? Are you still worried about us?"

"I worry about us everyday. You're the best thing in my life." She reached for my hand. "I'm still afraid I might lose you."

I was speechless. I, too, was worried everyday, if I was going to lose her. Or worse than that, have to leave her. I kissed the back of her hand, then leaned to kiss her forehead, and then her lips. I slowly stepped away, hesitating to leave at all. I stalled myself at the door and met her eyes in the dark. "I love you, girl," I said in a subtle voice, blowing her a kiss, as she returned one back to me. Moments later, I stood near my driver's side door and glanced back at the apartment's living room window. I shook my head with a guilty smile and drove away.

Breakdown

Where were my spiritual accountability partners when I needed them? I felt my body sinning and I didn't deter it from doing so. Who was holding me accountable when my flesh motivated me to lay with Lydea? No one. My college friends certainly wouldn't have taken that role seriously. They saw nothing wrong with my sinful acts. They gave me accolades when I told them my business. My friends' views on relationships were no different than how the rest of the world saw it. "Sex before marriage is what couples should do," they would say. *But if this were true, then why are there so many burdened teenagers and college students?* I wondered.

When I think about this worldly way of physical relationships between men and women, it contradicts what God says about it. Christ's disciple, Apostle Paul, speaks boldly in 1 Corinthians 6:13 on this topic by saying, *"The body is not for fornication, but for the Lord, and the Lord for the body."* The Bible reminds us to remain pure and save ourselves for marriage and there I was, pleasing my flesh, sinning without the fear of sin's consequences. Once again, I had to ask the Lord to forgive me of my lustful flesh. I couldn't deny my filthiness. I was so foolish back then. The only type of safe sex that exists outside of marriage is no sex at all. I wish I had gotten that through my thick skull.

~ My Exodus ~

30

Thursday morning arrived and I was ready for my trip to Atlanta. By early afternoon, Lydea and I finally got off the phone, which we had been on most of the morning. Our discussion wasn't about me leaving for the summer or her getting to New Jersey, but about Jason threatening to kill himself or the closest person to him. Lydea's voice shook franticly as she shouted into the phone.

"Jayden, you will not believe what's going on over here! I have to leave!"

"What's the matter? Where's Jason?" I pushed.

"He's here and he's lost his mind. That skank, Carla, told him what we did the other night in the room and he started goin' *loco*. He's been yelling in my face since earlier, saying I disrespected him. And just an hour ago, that jerk shoved me down the steps of the apartment and threw me outside!"

"What? Why?"

"I don't know. I don't know. I stepped out of the shower with my towel on, 'cause I thought he was at work, but then he snatched me up and threw me outside," she expressed rapidly. "I stood out there banging on the door for like ten minutes looking stupid, crying."

"We 'bouta fight," I roared, pacing the kitchen while my sister watched my reactions to Lydea's words. "Why was he trippin'?" I exploded. "*He said* I could stay there. That wasn't even the first time!"

"Exactly. The boy is crazy. You have no idea. He held the door shut from the inside, cursing at me. I was so embarrassed. Oh Lord, hold on one second, okay?" I waited for Lydea's attention, listening closely to her muffled voice as she covered the mouthpiece. "Jason, stop! Put it down!" she screamed. "Jayden, I'll call you right back. He has a knife."

"Wait! Lyd, don't hang up!" I heard a click, followed by dead silence. Oh my goodness. I couldn't believe the insanity that was going on just a few cities away. Why was she staying with him? I was praying to God that Jason wouldn't do anything stupid with that knife. I was fully aware of what he was capable of doing, so the worst was assumed. Within seconds, my phone rang again. It was Lydea, panicking.

"What am I gonna do?" she exclaimed with jumping nerves. "Jason just slit his forearm and blood is everywhere. I don't know what to do!"

"Are you serious? This ain't really happening." I continued to pace. "He hasn't touched you, has he?" I dared her to say yes, so I could get the cops involved.

"No. No. But he's been yelling at me all morning. What if he does something worse to himself? Jay, I don't know what to do. No one else is here."

"What if he does something worse to you?" I cried out. "You can't stay there, Lyd. Leave and get help!"

"What do I do?"

"I'm 'bouta call 911," I said, reaching for my house phone. My mind couldn't handle such madness.

"No! Don't," she demanded. "He has a problem, that's all. It comes and goes. I can help him. Jay, really—"

"His problems ain't your problems," I interrupted. "Open your eyes, Lydea! Call for help. He has a knife!"

"You don't understand. Jason gets mad because he can't have me, and when Carla told him that we had sex, he flipped. He's never acted out like this before. Not to this extreme, anyway. What—" she paused again. "He says he enjoys the pain he feels. He's lost it. I *have* to be here for him."

No matter how hard I tried, Lydea's feet were planted. We both knew that Jason was a negative influence in her life, but nothing was being done about it. By noon, my phone rang again. My daytime minutes were fried.

"Babe, I don't feel so good," my girl said, sickly.

"What's wrong? You need to lie down?"

"No, Jason's stitching his arm."

"Don't play with me right now," I said in disbelief.

"I'm not lying. He found some needle and thread in Carla's linen closet. He said that he hates the emergency room, so he's become his own doctor. The boy's insane."

Listening to her explain what Jason was doing with his open flesh was disturbing. I couldn't imagine what it was like for her to visualize it. He performed his surgery, laughing like a serial killer. While Lydea and I spoke, she held his stitches in place as he stuck himself with the needle.

"I feel like throwing up," she admitted in a weak tone.

It was unreal. My mind was being pulled and grinded like a thick rope in a tug of war. One side of me anticipated the drive to Atlanta and the other side wanted to drive to Norfolk and swoop up my lady.

Finally, by 2 p.m., my mother and sister said they were ready to head out, as they placed their last items in my Honda, which would be my transportation around the busy city. The three of us strapped our seat belts and voiced a prayer before leaving the driveway. I drove with my mind spiraling. I had no plans to speak with my mother about Lydea, but inevitably my girl's name soon popped up. I clarified her reasons for not being able to go back to Camden and to no surprise, my mother had trouble understanding. It was difficult enough for me to understand.

Throughout our journey, my aching girlfriend kept in touch with me. I contemplated how I was going to handle her living condition. My thoughts remained scrambled. While driving, I realized the severity of Lydea's dysfunctional lifestyle; a particular lifestyle that a lot of young adults can relate to. She was simply lacking a stable foundation. I tried my best to get others to show her mercy, but what did that accomplish? If I had been transparent with others about my relationship, they would've wondered why I stayed. At the time, I was more concerned about what others thought of me, so I hid the truth from them just to avoid their constructive criticism. My intention was to avoid giving Lydea a bad name, still I wasn't being honest with others or myself. I was burdened with an internal weight and shamefully became afraid of the truth.

Besides the intense dialogue my mother and I held in the car, our ride along Interstate 85 was smooth. Hours later, I pulled off the highway in Charlotte and veered into a gas station to fill up. Afterwards, I switched seats with my mother and flopped into the passenger's side. I reclined my seat back as far as it would go and closed my eyes to escape reality. While a relaxing CD of mine played quietly throughout the car speakers, I dozed off, embracing the lyrics of the song, "Good Girls," by the well-seasoned R&B artist, Joe.

The song filled my eyes with water, and before the song had ended I was fast asleep.

When my eyelids crept open after my long nap, my blurred vision caught a glimpse of our approaching exit. Sitting there, I thanked the Lord for watching over us as we traveled without accident or incident. I understood that God had a plan for my life, to give me a hope and a future. I was pleased in knowing that no obstacle had gotten in the way of my destination. While seated, my conscience spoke to Jesus. *Forgive me, Lord, of my past sins. My righteousness has been like filthy rags. I sincerely ask that you give me a fresh start and a renewed mind.* Pulling into my aunt's driveway at a quarter til' 11p.m., I said with confidence, "My sinful days are over."

I couldn't go back to my old sinful self again. I didn't recognize who I had become. I couldn't allow my flesh to control my spirit and damage my soul any longer. I didn't want to wrestle with my thoughts anymore. I needed God's wisdom to handle the relationship I was in. I wanted the Lord's will for my life and not my own. My Savior's love is incredible. He's a jealous God. He loved me even when I was putting him second. Even while I was sinning, Christ still loved me. His kindness led me to repentance. In my conviction, I verbally made a pledge to Jesus before I got out of the car that with his help, I would remain obedient in all his ways until his second coming. What a vow to make to God!

Breakdown

Obedience isn't always the easiest path to walk. Doing the right thing is often one of the most difficult procedures to perform, especially when another individual is doing wrong. But, through God's Word, I've learned that I don't struggle against flesh and blood, but rather against spiritual wickedness in high places (Eph. 6:12). Did my pride justify my wicked ways? Of course it did. My rebellion developed in my mind. That's why it was so hard to fight sin and tempting opportunities. My pride had me thinking that I could overcome the devil's schemes on my own, but I couldn't. I had to depend on Christ, my provider. For all those months, my obedience was being tested and I was blind to his kingdom. There's no compromising and debating with the King; we must obey the King.

Jesus said the greatest commandment is to love God (Mark 12:30). Then he said if we love him, we would obey him (John 14:15). Then the Bible goes on to parallel *not* obeying him with sin (James 4:17). How could I verbally say that I loved God, knowing that I was living a secret life of disobedience? If I tell God that I love him, I want him to believe my words. I don't want my lips to say one thing and my actions say another. It's so true—after salvation, spiritual, physical, and emotional obedience in its purest form is love in God's eyes. Obedience is what he wants!

~ Flood of Emotions ~

31

With my new verbal contract, there I was in Atlanta, thankful for another summer internship. It's amazing how this opportunity became available. At the time, my older cousin, Ricky, was a director at a successful family-owned residential company, and one of his draftsmen was given a surgery date on the second week of June and wasn't expected to return until August. Was it by chance that these were the exact months for my summer employment? No, simply God's grace.

My first week and a half was vacation, so one day while enjoying my Aunt Cheryl's outdoor pool, my competitive, younger cousin, Aaron and I took turns holding our breath under the water. The moment he went under, my cell rang. I motioned to the ledge and answered, "Yo, yo, yo."

"Hey, Jayden. It's me, Lydea." As if I had forgotten what her voice sounded like.

"Hey, girl, what's goin' on? Gimme some good news," I said pointing to the phone by my ear, looking at Aaron's wide grin.

"I'm lonely," she sulked. "I miss you."

"Aw, c'mon, babe. I've only been gone for four days."

"Well, it feels a lot longer than that. I wish you were still here. I really do miss you," she emphasized.

"You know I miss you too, girl. Hey, I meant to ask you, did everything calm down from last week?" I said, hoping for a short yes, but as the story prolonged and the topics switched, I cut her short. "Yo, Lyd, sorry, but can we finish this conversation after nine? My daytime minutes are real slim over here."

"Aww, Jay. There's no one else to talk to. I'm bored."

"I'm sure you are. That's why you need a job. Now, I'm willing to sacrifice my upcoming cell phone bill to chat with you if you *really* need me to, but this little casual conversation we're having right now ain't gonna put me in debt. Sorry, babe."

"Fine. Call me later. You still love me?"

"Yes, I still love you, girl. I'll call you later," I said.

"Okay. *Chao nene. Yo tambien te amo.*"

"Huh? I missed that last part. Slow down."

"I said, I love you too, boy," she translated. "Bye."

"Aight, girl. Bye."

That was my relationship, on and off the phone. My days on vacation all blended together—playing ball, swimming, eating, sleeping, reading, church, and talking on the phone. Soon enough, the whole house knew about my girlfriend and her living situation. I stood in the kitchen one morning and my aunt and uncle brought her name up. I began telling them the truth about my relationship, yet leaving much of it out. "Lydea's a wonderful girl," I told them holding a glass of orange juice. "She just needs more support from her family," I said, making a difficult circumstance seem easy. "And that's where I come in."

"What does her family have to do with you?" My Aunt Cheryl stepped in front of my uncle, waving a spatula. "Y'all aren't married. You can encourage her by being a godly friend. Your girlfriend is staying with a guy that likes her. That just doesn't sit well with me."

I argued back, "She's just staying with him until she finds a place of her own, that's all. I'm the only one pushing her in the right direction, back with her family."

My aunt rolled her eyes to meet with my uncle's. They both looked back at me and spoke in one accord, "What does her family have to do with you?"

"I don't know, but she needs me!" I raised my voice.

"She needs the Lord. Has she met him?" my spiritually inclined aunt questioned.

"Well, yeah. Sort of," I replied, knowing in my heart that Lydea wasn't saved. "Aunt Cheryl, you'd like her."

"I probably would," she agreed, placing the spatula down onto the island counter, next to a hot pan of cooking omelets. She rested both of her hands on my shoulders and stared dead into my eyes. "Jayden, you know what to do. Now is the time to do it."

Her words struck my ears with thunder. She was right. The ball was in my court and I had a choice to make. I knew what to do, but making the best decision for myself felt selfish. Lydea still needed me as her encourager. I was her friend, her true friend, but did she really need me as her boyfriend? In order to receive a true answer, I sought the Lord's voice.

After days of praying and fasting, my hearing was swiftly restored with Jesus. He spoke to me in several ways; first method being the Bible. It was just me and the pages of his Word. I highlighted scripture on the sofa where I sat, reading the books of 1 and 2 Corinthians quietly, which brought correction to my spirit. The second method that the Lord used to speak was through the chapters of a book entitled *The Purpose Driven Life* by the spirit-filled author and pastor, Rick Warren. The wisdom in Warren's words unlocked my understanding and gave clarity to my God-given purpose. The third means of communication was merely through a life group that my aunt and uncle both hosted at their house. The group was made up of members and non-members of the church, having fellowship and worship outside of the sanctuary walls.

That Friday evening, I hid amongst the unfamiliar faces, creating a generation gap. I was the youngest in the room, yet I sat with my ears wide open. God must've ordained the topic we spoke about because the word *obedience* was in bold letters, centered at the top of the sheets that were passed around. The group spoke plainly about being obedient to God and how they could avoid falling short. The mature advice that was given from the believers in the circle brought a different perspective to my young mind. Several men and women admitted their disobedient lifestyles, and asked for advice while I sat quietly on the couch and soaked it all in, asking God to keep speaking to me.

By the end of our gathering, we all stood and circled for prayer. God's presence fell heavily in the living room and burdens were lifted. With my eyes closed, I felt a tap on my shoulder. A few of the ladies wanted to pray for me. I was honored when the lead vocalist from the church held my hands high and prophesied over my life, reading Isaiah 11: 2–5: *"And the spirit of the Lord shall rest upon him, the spirit of wisdom and understanding, the spirit of counsel and might, the spirit of knowledge and fear of the Lord; And shall make him of quick understanding in the fear of the Lord: and he shall not judge after the sight of his eyes, neither reprove after the hearing of his ears: But with righteousness shall he judge the poor, and reprove with equity for the meek of the earth: and he shall smite the earth with the rod of his mouth, and with the breath of his lips shall he slay the wicked. And righteousness shall be the girdle of his loins, and faithfulness the girdle of his reins."*

My soul was humbled. It was difficult to receive such a high calling on my life. I read the verse over many times in my solitude to eat the fruit of the scripture. I don't remember much of the following day except for the conversation that Lydea and I held over the phone late that evening in my aunt's spacious main level master bedroom, a dwelling place that I considered mine.

During our dialogue, Lydea, still giggling, said, "Hey, if I tell you something, will you promise not to get mad?"

Oh no! My conscience wailed. *Not now. What could it be this time?* "What's wrong, Lyd? What happened?" I asked, avoiding her question.

"Don't get mad okay? I'm gonna tell you this because I think you should know." Her tone quickly became serious.

"You can talk to me," I said calmly, getting up from my seated position on the bed. "What's up?"

"Okay, well," she sighed, "you remember the night Jason held me down?"

"Yeah," I replied, searching through my top dresser draw for a clean pair of boxers. "I really don't wanna think about it, but go ahead."

"And you know how me and you had sex the night before?"

"I mean, I guess. Why?" I asked, baffled. "Round the bases, Lyd. What are you trying to say?"

"Well, um—I'm late. So I checked to see if I was—well, you know, pregnant. And I took the test a few days ago and it says—I am. But I didn't think it was right, so I took it again, and it's saying the same thing…. Jayden, I'm scared. I am so scared right now, I don't know what to do."

Sniffling as she spoke, Lydea confessed a different kind of honest surprise that shocked the life out of me. I hesitated to speak. "Don't be scared," I comforted. "If you are then—we can work this out. I'm not gonna run from this situation. When are you planning to see the doctor?"

"First thing Monday."

"Okay, we'll see what the doctor has to say," my voice lowered. "Don't worry, babe. It'll be fine. I'm here for you, all right?"

"But, one more thing. If the doctor confirms that I am, I already know my decision."

"I-I don't understand," I stuttered.

"I'm going to have the abortion."

"What? Why?" I disagreed. "What for?"

"Jayden, because, this might not be yours!" she cried. "I'm not gonna have Jason's child! I don't know what to do. I wish you were here."

"What if I am the father?" I inquired.

"And what if you're not?" she sobbed over the phone while my stomach twisted like a strong tornado. After the terrible truth was announced, I left her with consoling words and excused myself from the phone.

Shortly after, I stood in the shower and let the heated streams of water ease the internal pain of disappointment that stung like a thousand bees. The hot water cleansed me physically, but emotionally and spiritually, I felt so dirty. I prayed and cried, and cried and prayed, silently shouting to God, *What kind of relationship have I gotten myself into? My own girlfriend doesn't even know who she's pregnant by! This isn't the life I want, Lord! Take this burden from me. I don't want this life, God!*

Horrible thoughts from prior months shook me all at the same time, one after the other. All my insecurities, worries, and doubts slapped me in my face, taunting, "We told you so." The burning feeling that shot through my bones was awful. I was infuriated, but I couldn't be mad at her. How could I hold a grudge against Lydea? She was raped, held down and taken advantage of. Jason, on the other hand, made me sick. I hated hearing his name or anything that concerned him. He was the seed of our problems. But above him, there was someone who kindled my fire even more, and it was the devil himself, my real enemy.

The next morning at my aunt's large church, I was prepared to receive a word from the pastor and only by the agreement of the Holy Spirit was his sermon on obedience. I knew this was Jesus' supernatural way of speaking to me again. While the pastor taught the congregation, a few women fixed their hair, and a few men looked around as if their full attention wasn't on him. I, on the other hand, was the complete opposite. My hearing was inclined. I listened to his every word. "It's me and you, Lord," I mumbled, projecting loud enough for my cousin, Aaron, to hear me. "Keep on talking to me," I said softly. "Keep on talking to me, Jesus. Your servant is listening."

In my spirit, I felt that this was the fulfillment of my prayers, the reason behind my relationship, and the testing of my faith. Lydea and I made a wonderful couple, the type that folks admired, nevertheless, Sunday's message was confirmation that I had to sever our bond. It pierced me like a sharpened arrow. I had to end our relationship. God wanted me to return to him fully. *Come back to your first love,* he said to my soul. At the end of service, I raised my hands along with the majority of the congregation and surrendered to God without further delay.

Breakdown

That day in church, I was positive that God was not only confirming what he had desired of me from the beginning, but I was confident in hearing his voice when he told me to end my relationship with Lydea. All the other breakups were on me, but the Lord had appointed this one. My emotions were stirred. How could I break our bond again, knowing that she was leaning towards having an abortion? With all the reasons I had to delete her title, I didn't want to add any more pain to her heart. I knew that breaking up wouldn't be an easy thing to do, although I had done it several times before. What was my problem? Maybe I thought I was supposed to accomplish more of my purpose. Maybe I thought the two of us were supposed to have a different ending. I didn't know what to think. My thoughts were knotted in one large ball. All I could do was follow through in obedience and see what God had planned next. If I was all that Lydea had, then my heart goes out to her because I no longer was.

~ Number Five ~

32

That Sunday evening, I spoke with Lydea outside of my aunt's house and broke off our relationship for the final time. It felt like the first one back in October was connected to this last one. The second, third, and fourth split-ups were all bricks being added to our wall of insecurity. The purpose of a wall is to divide and separate, right? So with my heart surrounded by bricks, I stood on my decision to break off my relationship as Lydea opposed.

"What do you mean?" she screamed through the phone. "Jayden, what did I do?"

"I gotta do it."

"Tell me what I did? We were talking fine last night. Please, don't do this to me again. I need you. Why are you doing this?" she said, wondering why I was pushing her away for the fifth time. "Can't you see that I need you? My life has gotten outta control! You can't leave me now. Not now!" she cried.

"What do you want me to say?" I shrugged, hoping to keep my answers brief.

"Answer me. What did I do?" she shouted. "Tell me what I did? You know I didn't do anything wrong. Tell me!"

"Man, it's—it's—it's everything! What haven't you done?" I blasted. "Everything from our past, where you're staying, how you're living—all that trash has pushed me to do this. Your boy is the number one reason! He's always been the reason. It makes me so mad knowing that I'm here in Atlanta with my family and my girlfriend is living in Virginia with some backstabber, who she considers her friend. He ain't your friend, Lydea! I've told you that before."

"What do you want me to do?" she roared, as I paced the lengthy driveway.

"I don't know what you're gonna do, but I ain't puttin' up with this three-way relationship any more," I told her. "That's what I do know. Believe me when I say this, ending our relationship isn't because of one or two things. It's a long list of everything."

"No! No, Jayden. I told you that I've changed. I told you from the beginning of our relationship that Jason means nothing to me. I've grown to hate him. I even asked you last year if you wanted me to get rid of him, and you told me no. I blame him too for our relationship being what it is. Just understand that I wouldn't be in this apartment if I had somewhere else to go. I have no family to run to. I don't have the perfect family like you do. Why are you holding that against me? I have nowhere else to go!"

Our aggressive conversation went on for hours, well past midnight. I eventually said good-bye to her and bitterly hung up. The following morning was my first day as an intern and despite my lack of sleep, my anticipation sprung me out of bed early that same morning.

The first day on the job went great. I was introduced to the guys in the department and several others around the office building. Working there was one hundred times better than being a cashier at a busy pet store. This was the type of job I knew my college degree could get me. Sitting at my desk near a window, put a smile on my face. Working in the home building industry had always been a dream of mine, and there I was, living out my dream.

By lunchtime, my phone began to vibrate. Several text messages filled with inquisition bombarded my cell, hitting one after the other. They were all coming from Lydea, my ex-girlfriend. I countered with, "I'll call you later."

Leaving from work at 5 p.m., she called me before I could call her. We chatted and debated briefly. "Hey, I gotta watch my minutes," I said. "They're not free until after nine. I'll call you back, okay?" By 7 p.m., she called again. She wanted answers and she wanted them from my mouth. Once I returned the call at 9 p.m., I did more listening than talking. When I spoke, the words from my lips all sounded similar, echoing my point from the night before.

I held the phone away from my ear, resting from her complaints. In my conscience I began to wonder, *Did I introduce Lydea to Jesus? Did I edify her even a little bit? Was I Christ-like at all?* I knew every time my flesh became a priority over my spirituality, Satan's presence was near, but I persisted. I thought I had disappointed God because I didn't walk in the fullness of what he had asked of me. My lustful desires became a reflection of my past relationships. I acknowledged that I wasn't deep enough in the Bible or in prayer to overcome the temptation that presented itself to me those multiple times, but I persisted. I depended on the Holy Spirit to guide my steps in truth. It was my self-control and discipline that was lacking. My full obedience to God's spoken commandment had fallen short, but I persisted. I then placed the phone back to my ear and began recalling the heart breaking occasions that took place between the two of us. Even the mishaps that I thought were forgiven and swept under the rug from months ago were immediately uncovered.

"Why are you killing me with questions?" I asked out of resentment, stretched across the king size bed, wanting to hang up. "You don't want my damn love, remember?"

"Jayden, stop it. I didn't mean that."

"Did you mean it when you told me to shut the hell up in front of your boy and everyone else in the library? Huh?"

"Stop already. That was a long time ago. I've changed. You know that."

The two of us spoke for hours that night. In the background, I could hear Jason laughing at the television program they were watching. I'm sure he knew the topic of our discussion. But before we got off the phone, Lydea posed one last suggestion.

"Jay, work with me on this, okay? I need your support. My friend, Arnold, from high school lives in Hampton now, and he got me to the doctor today, but I'm scheduled for the abortion on Thursday. Could we at least postpone our breakup until I go to the clinic? I've never done something like this before."

I knew she needed me as a crutch. She wanted my love as well as my friendship, but my head was filled with too much clutter. I couldn't believe that a part of me might've been growing inside of her. *What if* that was my baby? *What if* I was the father of the miracle in her womb? Would the baby have looked more like Lydea or me? My mind was consumed with questions, and sleep didn't come easy.

Although we remained apart, our text messages and phone calls were still daily. My daytime minutes were without a doubt much higher than what my plan allowed. Strangely, our talk time had increased since the initial breakup a week before. Our conversations were strictly my answers to her questions. We were no longer a couple, yet our talk time proved otherwise. I remained steadfast about this fifth and final relational collapse. I had no intentions of hooking any U-turns. My focus was on the Lord.

Breakdown

Was it abnormal for Lydea and I to keep in contact while being exes? I wasn't planning on being her man again, so I don't know why I continued to answer her calls. My feelings were scattered. My emotions were displaced. When she spoke, I listened. When I spoke, she spoke. That's how most of our dialogues carried on. Many nights, she bluntly expressed how she felt, but other nights she was reserved and kept to herself. Out of compassion, I continued to listen to her troubled heart. I prayed for her situation, hoping that God would uproot her from the quicksand that she was stuck in.

While Lydea attempted to reel me back in, I pressed on, forgetting those things that were behind me. The moment I gave my love life back to Jesus, I didn't have to deal with my relational sins and problems anymore. They had become too much of a distraction and a load. I had avoided wise counsel for too long. An old man once told me, "There is no one more blind than someone who will not listen to good advice." I say Amen to that. A crooked thumbs up was mine from day one.

~ The Dog Days of Summer ~

33

Throughout the week, I kept my phone close to my hip in case Lydea had any breaking news to pass on. Regardless of our status, the phone calls were expected.

"Jay, I hate it here," she expressed. "Jason's been treating me so bad lately."

"Sounds like Newton's Third Law."

"What? What's that supposed to mean?"

"Newton's Third Law," I said, driving. "I mean, you've been telling me how much you hate Jason's guts, and how sick you are of him, and he hears nearly every back stabbing word you say. Every action has an equal but opposite reaction. I passed physics, you know."

"For one, you're using it out of its original context, and two, I don't care if he hears me or not. It's the truth."

"Well, as much as I object to talking behind folks back, in your case, it might be best if you did. This is probably why he's been treating you the way he has."

"Who knows? He's not here now. I don't care," Lydea said. "Did I tell you last week that he pushed me out the bed?"

"Last week? No."

"Yeah, last Tuesday he told me to pack all my things."

"Why am I hearing about this now?"

"You were too busy to talk last week, remember? But like I was saying, he was throwing pillows and shoes at me. First thing in the morning! Then he stood over me while I was getting up from off the floor and started swinging."

"He hit you?" I asked in shock.

"No, *he hugged me.* Yes, he hit me!"

"What?" I knew the two of them scuffled occasionally, but this act of madness was uncommon.

Lydea continued, "My bottom lip was swollen in two spots from where he slapped me. But I feel good 'cause I scratched his face off. I sliced him right across his cheekbone. Aren't you proud of me?"

What can I do four states away? My mind raced with vengeance as I pulled into a gas station for an expensive fill up. "I don't even know what to say right now," I hesitated. "But thanks for telling me 'cause you know what? I'm 'bouta call the cops right now on his—"

"No," she interrupted. "Don't do that."

"What! Are you defending him?" I yelled. "Who can that punk hit with handcuffs on, Lydea? Don't stop me from saving you. Don't do this again."

"I'm fine. It's not that serious."

"I don't care," I said with a clenched jaw. "I'm callin' the cops on your boy and he deserves whatever they give him. I'm tired of this. Don't stop me from doing what's right. Get the police involved. Do it!"

"I'm all right. It's not like I need stitches or anything. I'll be fine," she said, deceiving herself.

"It's not all right! You won't be fine. Stop pretending like this is supposed to happen. Why haven't you left yet, girl? This is making me so mad 'cause you don't even *want* me to help you."

"I'll handle it, Jayden. Really, it's fine."

I gave my advice until my advice ran out. I pushed for justice until I couldn't push any longer. I continued to be supportive; however, my support ended the day my phone service was cut off. As I had mentioned before, my talk time was beyond what my minutes had allowed. One afternoon while sitting at my desk at work, my cell phone rang. It was a service representative.

"Mr. Rockaway?" she asked.

"Yes. This is he," I answered.

"Hello sir, my name is Angela and I'm calling on behalf of your cell phone provider. I don't know if you're aware of your account status, but you have an astronomical bill, sir."

Whoa! That's a college word for ya, I thought. Who uses a term like *astronomical* to describe a cell phone bill? I was afraid to ask the lady how much I owed because I didn't want my day to be ruined. Seconds after we hung up, I called my mother in Virginia and asked her to investigate this for me. Waiting to hear back from her, I prayed hard, asking God to make it a manageable figure. I certainly didn't want to spend all of my hard earned internship money on a stupid bill that could've been avoided. It was true that Lydea and I spent a great quantity of time either talking or texting one another during that cycle, so I was prepared for the worst. But I should've been sitting down when my mother called me back later that evening.

"Jayden, I feel like crying," she trembled.

"Oh nah. Mom, are you serious? What did they say?" I asked, while getting ready for my Friday night small group.

"It's up there with tuition money!"

"Stop playing!" I shouted back. "How much did they say, Mom? Tell me."

"I can't believe this. Jay, they said $3,100!" she said, emphasizing every syllable of the total.

My mouth dropped and my throat became awfully dry. My summer income was shot. I felt like fainting. Did she say $3,100? "How did it go sky-high like that?" I asked doubtful.

"They said you've been roaming since the end of May. Plus, their information shows that you went *waaay* over your minutes."

I began to calculate in my head the length of time that I had been in Georgia, times three hours everyday of roaming. Even my free nights and weekends were being accounted for. Oh, how my heart hurt. I knew that I couldn't pay it all, and I surely couldn't ask Lydea to help me.

The next day, I explained to the manager over the phone, "Ma'am, I remember changing my service plan from local to nationwide at the beginning of May. So, for me to have been roaming during this period is definitely arguable."

Hours later, my service was cut off. Days after that, it was sporadically back on, then off again. Then for a half a dozen straight days, my phone was lifeless. I remained in prayer, hoping that God was willing to at least knock off most of the debt.

By the end of June, another representative called me on my work phone. "Mr. Rockaway, the roaming charges that increased your bill to the current amount, is our mistake," the gentleman said. "We have on file that you requested a plan change on the first of May, so we do apologize for that error, sir. However, the charges for exceeding your allotted minutes still remains," he concluded.

I was relieved when he told me the recalculated amount, which was much lower than the original. Nevertheless, I continued to pray. "My Lord, will you please remove this mountain of a bill from me? Bless me with a free bill?" I asked humbly on my knees that night. "You know my situation, Lord. Lydea and I were breaking up and she needed to speak with me, Father. Please don't punish me financially for all I've done. Forgive me for any wrong I've committed, Lord. You said that if I abide in you and you abide in me, then I can ask for whatever I desire and you'll give it. Can you *please* remove this mountain from me?" I pleaded with passion, trusting that God was listening to my fervent prayer.

A few days later, my mother called me at the job and gave me the update on my cell phone bill.

"Hey, how's my darling son?" she pleasantly asked.

"I could be better, Ma," I replied in a depressed tone. "Do you have any good news for me?"

"Well, this is very strange, but I just got off the line with Angela, the agent who spoke with you the other week, and she explained to me that they dropped *all* the charges, due to the mishaps that were made on their behalf. But not only that, somehow she said you'll have a credit of $73!"

I jumped up from my office desk, shocked as could be. "How do they owe me money?" I exclaimed.

"Don't ask," my mom replied.

"I won't," I said, as my three co-workers all stared in my direction.

In complete gratitude, I gave God praise for sprinkling his grace on me. Not only was I overjoyed with the great news about my bill, but my disabled phone service blocked all communication between Lydea and I. Our friendship was distant and our relationship was beginning to fade.

Breakdown

What a summer! So many accounts, not enough paper. During an open mic night at my Uncle Isles' small church, I was given an opportunity to tell the audience what the Lord had done. In between my two spoken-word pieces, I gave my testimony. A sky-high bill dropping to negative $73 is such a demonstration of how God can move mountains with just the faith of a mustard seed. I'm not lying.

I sent Lydea a text message about my good news, but she down played my story and replied, "Jayden, I never want to experience another year like this ever again. My life sucks. My father has a blood clot in his brain and he's going to need surgery. I hate my life."

My sympathy remained. Of all the possibilities that were once hopeful back in May, not one had come to pass. A new apartment? No. Her car back? Negative. A new job? Not even close. Now her father was having health issues? I wanted to bring it all up during our text message conversations, but I couldn't add hot coals to the fire. She needed to hear words of encouragement and hope. Yet, she couldn't understand why I continued to edify her, being her ex. I didn't have an answer either. I guess I was still stuck on accomplishing what God had commanded of me from the beginning.

~ Blood for Ink ~

34

Our inconsistency over the telephone was a positive inconvenience as I stood on my decision to remain single. It would've been nearly impossible to be obedient to God and myself if I went back to the relationship that God himself was trying to tear apart. In the early half of July, I restricted myself from returning Lydea's phone calls. Even our text messages became a thing of the past. In one of the several messages that were left on my voicemail, she told me to expect a letter in the mail from her. *Hmm, a letter?* I thought. *Not a bad alternative.* So with nothing to lose, I darted to my aunt's basement and sat at the computer and expressed my heart through the keyboard. My letter to Lydea was typed as follows:

These last few weeks have been hard. How can mental pain hurt worse than physical scars? It's even harder to explain. The pain that fills my bones everyday is the same pain that won't go away. But understand what kind of pain I'm talking about. It's the same pain that resulted in me pushing you away. Don't ever think I'm insane or on the verge of stupidity. Many times my cup (my thoughts) overflows with breakup agility. This means that I think about bouncing because

I don't have the most stable relationship. It almost reminds me of Bobby and Whitney's, excluding the drugs.

There hasn't been a night that we didn't talk about our love, or what I thought it was. Yes, I've proclaimed it to you many nights. Night after night, I actually meant the words that rolled off my tongue. Yet I found myself using the same tongue to say that our love isn't right. Do you know how long it took me to win you over? This is a relationship, not a roller coaster. Many times, your cold ways had me red hot like a toaster. But I cooled off, remember? I think it was last October; no, it was November; no, it was December. Yes, last December you promised me I had nothing to worry about. The word *worry* means concern, to lose sleep, be bothered, be troubled with. The word *nothing* means not anything, zip, zero, zilch. Why am I still wondering when you're going to move out?

Lydea, you see my love for you is more than just a slow song or some roses. The devil himself could tell me that he loves me, but I would have to be the one to oppose it. Love is not a word that you can agree to say at the end of every conversation. It's not a word that you learn through education. Was this why you were so afraid to fall in love all this time? Did you know how much it would hurt your mind? How bad does this hurt your heart? How much does this touch your soul? I thought about you everyday, faithfully, like you were my favorite piece of gold. I always wondered how my precious jewel started looking dull. I took care of you as well as I could, until my jewel sparkled in full. I would ask you questions like, "If I'm doing everything right, then why are you fading on me?" You would respond by saying, "Don't worry about that. I'm not doing anything wrong. You know that I love you, right, baby?" Come to find out another man was given the time to make my jewel dirty. My one and only jewel being destroyed by someone so unruly. I looked so foolish. My insides looked even worse. I had to listen to my girl tell someone else that she loves them. Who's being put first? I have a dry throat writing this because my heart hurts. The reasons for all the breakups were my way of escaping. I was too weak of a man, so I began faking that I could be strong enough to let this movie continue taping.

I feel like crying. Not a second after writing the word cry, my eyes filled up with tears. Not one fell because I'm Simply Red, still holding back the years. I'm still holding on to my fear of loving someone who doesn't love me in return (not saying that you don't). There's one thing that I've learned about myself from past relationships: I've never been one to fight or cuss, but I'll cuss and fight if the one I love doesn't love me as much. And yes, it's a fight within myself. I have only shown you fragments of my anger. You have barely heard whispers of my rage. I used to wonder what was holding you back from releasing me from my cage. I mean, what kind of strong hold has been on you to just stand outside of my kennel and look at me as if you wanted to own me, but never taking me? What took you so long to take me out and touch me? When you held me in your arms, it felt so right. But soon enough, I was put back in isolation as you turned and walked away. Then you would return the next day to repeat your actions. I would jump for joy every time I saw you at my cage. I felt like you wanted to take me home with you, but there was something stopping you, some force or some wall. I was all yours from the beginning, but I had to wait and wait and wait for you to want me as much as I wanted you. It's gotten to the point where I've felt your touch and have been around you so many times that I fell in love with you. Yet I questioned why I was still in my cage. People told us that we look so good together, but my ownership was unannounced. Now, all of a sudden, you want to love me and take me home. You're ready for a companion who you can call your own. Unfortunately, I've relocated and changed for the better. Oh, why does our relationship have to be filled with bad weather? Liquid Sunshine is what I'd call it. The sun would shine so bright until the rain would spoil it.

My love for you will always be different. Is this what we meant by being on separate pages? You know that I speak in parables, in such ways that you may not be able to overstand, but I understand them perfectly. Many nights I had to search deep down inside of me. I'm grateful that the Lord God Almighty is a close friend of mine. I talk to him out loud while he speaks to my heart, spirit, soul, and mind. I ask questions and my Father in heaven answers. I find my thoughts choreographed like my spirit is a professional dancer. My feet won't stop moving to the movement of my melody. I'm following God's purpose for my life without any love felonies. No more love crimes being committed and me being offended. There are so many things to mention, but not enough time to spend on them. The only thing I was spending was the feelings that I was lending.

Is a man a failure if he sends his heart through the mail and receives a delayed response? Did my package get lost? Why did it take you so long to open your package of love? Honestly, it might be too late now to respond to my love. My love was a gift that was unappreciated. You even threw it back at me, saying you didn't want my damn love. Those words still echo in my halls of emptiness, along with my lonely hugs. Don't ever think that you were the only one in this relationship. Don't ever think that the love wasn't mutual. Don't question my love for you because it's not up for discussion. I have strength to move past the past. I have the faith to know that I'm walking down the path of a bright future. Today is a gift; that's why I treat it like a present.

Lydea, you deserve gold that will never get dull or rusted. If you keep your favorite jewel close to you, make sure that no one else touches it. If you lose your jewel, try your hardest to find it. If you lose your lover, don't try your hardest to find him. God has a wonderful way of being a great matchmaker. Maybe if we had prayed together, our structure would've been more stable. Only through Him are we able. Are you able and willing to make your lover a being that is invisible? I've never seen Him or touched Him, but I know how He feels. He will make love to your heart and soul better than any man who is visible. I desperately wanted you to ask me for spiritual guidance when we were together. I desired for us to hold long conversations about our views on God and the Bible. What do you think the reason for your Christmas present was? I truly wish that you find someone who treats you like I did and can duplicate my love. Maybe if I'm fortunate, I will find the same. If we ever rekindle our love, beforehand would have to be major change. You have me thinking down the road. When you graduate, Atlanta is only 575 miles away. It has been known for people to save themselves for people because guess what, Rockaway isn't a bad last name...

Love,

Jayden Rockaway

Breakdown

My heart pumped blood for ink as I typed the letter. The moral behind it was, "After all we've been through, I forgive you, and I'm still here." I was trying to love unconditionally, although my conditional love for her succeeded.

Reading over the letter, the Holy Spirit opened my eyes and revealed to me that this was how the world treats God, keeping him caged and visiting occasionally. I immediately repented, because I, too, had put God in a box; one that he's never claimed to abide in. I'm guilty of putting a lid on God's limitless ability and matchless supremacy.

A week later, God proved himself once again by returning the letters that Lydea and I had written. Was this the Lord's way of stopping our feelings from being shared? If so, then I accepted his decision to keep my heart distant from hers. He's even in control of the mail that circulates around the world! God is truly a sovereign God.

~ God's Grace and Mercy ~

35

The month of August had arrived and my internship was coming to a quick end. I was five working days away from leaving a job that I had grown to appreciate and be thankful for. One afternoon, during lunch, my boss and first cousin, Ricky, pulled me aside and gave me an offer I couldn't refuse.

"Hey, Jay-Crew," he said gripping my shoulder, standing high over me with his thick mustache. "I've been wanting to speak with you about something. You got a minute?"

"Yeah, now is fine. You want to talk in your office?" I asked while drinking the last of my lemonade in the break room.

"As a matter of fact, yeah," Ricky replied. "Follow me." I trailed him down the hall and entered his office. "Shut the door for a second," he said sitting down. "I have good news and not so good news. Well, for you it's all good news. I spoke with Thomas this morning and he said he'd be back from his surgery this upcoming Monday. That's the good. But, it just so happens that I had to let Samuel go today, due to his lack of everything."

"Sam got fired?"

"Shhhh," Ricky motioned. "Yes. I gave him a lot of chances. Never mind that though. I want to let you know that there's now an open position in my department." Ricky paused. "Would you be willing to work for me after you cross that stage in December? You've got a lot of potential, my friend. Whatcha think?"

Bashfully grinning, I stood before him with my right hand extended, ready to confirm the deal. "I think you'll have a new draftsman come January, sir!" I told him with a bright smile, humbled by God's favor.

Opposite of my good news, many miles away in Norfolk, Lydea's situation still hadn't improved. She surprised me with a phone call that night and shared with me her woes. "Jayden, I'm so hungry," she moaned.

"It's after ten o'clock, girl. Why haven't you eaten yet?" I asked, watching TV, enjoying a bowl of ice cream on the sofa with my cousin, Aaron.

"There's an echo in the fridge over here. I haven't eaten anything in two days! *Normally* Jason would bring food home after work, but lately he hasn't given me anything. Jay, I've already lost twelve pounds this summer. I can't afford to lose any more."

"Dang. Twelve pounds ain't no joke. That's crazy."

"I know. Tell Jason that."

"I ain't telling that dude nothin'."

"Oh, I didn't tell you," she added. "Jason was scheduled to appear in court this past week, but he purposely missed it because he knew he was guilty. Ain't that stupid?"

"That *was* dumb. Anybody that runs from the law eventually gets caught. We all know that. Was it over drugs?" I wondered, fully aware of his lawless lifestyle.

"No, reckless driving. I was in the car when he got the ticket. I kept telling him to go to the courthouse, but it's too late now. That was so stupid of him," she emphasized. "I guess he likes being in trouble with the law."

"Yep, another brother lost," I agreed. "How sad it is. But hey, don't feel sorry for that man. Let God deal with him. At the end of the day, all you can do is pray for him."

The following week was at hand and I was no longer an intern. My family drove down for a few days and stayed at my Aunt Cheryl's house with me. The group of us ate out frequently at Atlanta's more familiar restaurants, spending way too much money on food. I even witnessed my parents holding hands and laughing together, something I hadn't seen in a while. *Happily married*, I thought to myself, admiring their marathon-like friendship. Riding through the city with my family, I thought of Lydea and Jason, curious as to how they were making it. Ironically, before I could even ask, she called to inform me.

"Jayden!" she yelled into the phone, "Jason's gone. What am I supposed to do?"

"What do you mean, he's gone?" I questioned.

"He left like twenty minutes ago! His job fired him late this afternoon, and the cops are here for him now. I don't know what he did, but he said he wasn't coming back."

"Slow down, girl," I said, trying to understand her.

"And Carla said I gotta be out by Monday. I gotta find somewhere to go! Jayden, you gotta help me. I barely have any money to my name. Plus, my uncle called and said that my father fell into a coma from his surgery. I'm begging you," she cried.

"Are you serious?"

"Yeah, my uncle's at the hospital with him now. What should I do? School starts next week, but I love my papa. What should I do?"

"I can't believe your pops is in a coma," I said shaking my head. "Family comes before school, Lyd. It has to. I say you go back home and be with your dad."

"I don't wanna withdraw though. I can't withdraw. I need to finish school. If I go back to Camden, I'll never get my degree."

"Don't say that."

"It's true. If I take a semester off, my stepmom is gonna make me work some low-paying job, answering phones to help with the bills. I'm a senior this year. I'm the only one in my family that's been to college. I can't drop out like this. It's not me!"

"Lyd, I understand. Believe me, I do. But do what makes sense. Carla's kickin' you out on Monday, and your father needs you. I know ya'll don't have the best relationship, but you can't miss this opportunity to be there for him. He's your blood."

"Jayden, please! You don't understand. No one understands," she spoke with fire. "My father might die and my mother's already dead. School is the only thing I have going for me. I'm so confused. If something happens to my dad it would be like reliving my mom's death all over again."

"Okay, calm down. Maybe I don't understand. But what if God has a bigger purpose for your life right now then finishing school?" I encouraged. "We don't know what the future holds. You might even get a degree from a better school. Who knows? College is all about timing and circumstance. You know that."

"I *want* to graduate. Not three years from now, not five, but next year. Ugh! This is killing me. I really want to graduate, but I love my father. Ooh," she grunted with aggravation, "God better have a plan for me, Jay, I swear."

Moments of utter silence hung in the air. I sat in the backseat with my siblings, waiting for her next words. My family could tell by our conversation that Lydea was in another quandary.

"Jay, when you get back to Virginia, can you please help me move out?" she sorrowfully asked.

"Yeah," I slowly agreed. My verbal agreement meant that I'd have to see her one last time, but was I ready to see my past love again? Was I truly over her? Could I stand next to her and hold a conversation without flirting? I contended with many weaknesses, but only time would tell.

My final days in Atlanta ended peacefully with my family. Sadly though, we knew that Virginia was calling. By Sunday morning, the five of us headed for Interstate 85. My brother and I took turns steering my Accord, and my father handled the rental car with my mother and sister. The Lord's angels watched over us as we safely made it back to Newport News in one piece.

Breakdown

It's so aggravating to know that the choices and decisions we make on good faith will either steer our legs down the right or wrong path. The scary thing is, we don't have any say in the outcome of our choices. May, June, July, and half of August was all it took for Lydea's life to be changed forever. Was it the thrown punches? The abortion? Or was it the days and nights with nothing to eat? I can't imagine breakfast, lunch, and dinner being absent for days at a time, unless I was purposely fasting.

I wish I knew her full story. My eyes were not her eyes. My pain was not her pain. My life was not her life. How could I forget to mention her father's life or death condition? Although I pointed Lydea in the right direction numerous times, for a complete season, I was happy to hear that she was willing to be with her father in his time of recovery.

In life, I've learned that words of direction are great, but add this to your wisdom box: most individuals want you to walk with them through life. This can be one of the hardest and most challenging things to do, yet one of the most rewarding.

~ Her Exodus ~

36

I woke up early the next morning with Lydea on my mind. I couldn't shake the thought of seeing her again. She was concerned about withdrawing from school, and I was anticipating my ninth and final semester at New Norfolk University. We were complete opposites of each other. A hundred thoughts zipped through my mind as I drove through the Hampton Roads Bridge Tunnel.

The feeling of pulling into their apartment complex felt strange, as if I were picking Lydea up for the very first time. I crept through the parking lot and was shocked to see her standing outside on the stoop, nicely dressed, waiting for my arrival. I pulled close to the curb; she opened the door and sat herself down.

"Good morning," I said, hoping for a smile.

"Hey," she replied with her head down, giving me a second and third glance before I stretched my arms to greet her with a tight hug. Her frame was much thinner than what I had remembered, but I didn't let her know. She was already aware of her weight loss and I'm sure she didn't need a reminder.

Once we arrived on campus we went our separate ways. I stood in my advisor's office and studied my class arrangement. I organized my free time around my new schedule and made it a daily routine. My college days were set up like clockwork, a circle—a cycle, to be exact. My phone rang as I stood there, surrounded by old classmates.

"Hello?" I answered.

"Hey, where are you? We agreed on eleven o'clock," the same voice that I had once fallen in love with said.

"I know. I'm leaving the Tech Building now."

"Well, I'm already at your car. Plus I need to get a few things from the store, all right? So hurry up."

"Okay, okay. I'm on my way. Gimme a few minutes."

After leaving campus, I drove Lydea to the nearby Wal-Mart in Norfolk, still low on words. I let her out in front of the store and waited for her return. 10 minutes later, she was back.

"We can go now," she said. "I have what I need."

"Where are we going?" I asked, clueless.

"The apartment," she snapped. "Where else?"

"I don't know," I said with an attitude, driving away. "How am I supposed to know where you need to go?"

"Jayden, today is not the day. Don't. Just don't," she said, buckling her seatbelt, filled with tension.

What kind of favor am I doing? I thought, feeling like her personal taxi cab driver. Nevertheless, if a taxi cab driver was what she needed of me, then so be it. I merged back onto the highway and headed towards the apartment.

"Hey," she said in a gloomy tone, "you know I'm gonna need a lot of help today, right?"

"Really? Nah, I didn't know," I sarcastically replied with my eyes locked on the road.

"I have a lot of clothes and shoes and stuff so—we might have to take a few trips in your car, if that's okay. I'll give you gas money if you need it," she offered.

"Nah, that's cool. Keep your money," I told her, surfing through the radio stations to ease my mind. "What are you gonna do with all your things?" I asked.

"Well, yesterday, I called Jason's sister and asked if I could use her spare closet," Lydea replied, "but it can only hold a little bit of what I have. Plus, Greyhound limits the number of bags the passengers can bring on, so I'm really screwed. What am I supposed to do with everything that's left over? Jay, my whole life's in that apartment."

"It'll be fine. We'll do the best we can. I know this is hard for you, but I need you to be strong today, aight?"

I listened to her sulk. I knew my support was the best way to aid her through that humbling day. Once we got to the apartment, we walked through the living room and sidestepped the personal substance that was scattered about.

"What's goin' on, y'all?" I directed towards Carla and Anthony, who sat on their new, used sofa, surrounded by open bottles of liquor and two cigarette butt-filled ashtrays. "It's good to see y'all are still together," I said, glancing at Jason's punched holes in the wall.

Immediately, the eerie feeling of being in his room jumped all over me again. My imagination began painting the episodes that were recorded by Jason and Lydea over the summer. *If only these walls could talk*, I said to myself, trying to remain focused on why I was there. I stood in the doorway as my eyes scanned the room. I hadn't seen such a mess in a very long time. Lydea was far from being packed. Her clothes, shoes, sheets, pillows, and blankets were spread all over, from the window to the wall.

"What happened to all the boxes and bags you had back in May?" I wondered.

"Ha. Don't ask," she shot back, sorting through her clothes. "The morning Jason threw his *loco* tantrum, he destroyed all but two boxes. He ripped *every* bag I had. All I have now are these two suitcases, this huge backpack, that treasure chest over there, and this box of trash bags."

"Dang. That dude needs to get checked out for real. Something is seriously wrong with him. And something is seriously wrong with you for having all these clothes!" I criticized. "Start making some decisions, girl. It's already going on one."

"I can't," Lydea said, flustered. "I'm stuck between a rock and a hard place. How can I choose what's worth taking, leaving, or throwing away?"

"By making a decision. Only so much can go on the Greyhound," I said, sloppily folding her sheets. "You have two large suitcases and a backpack *big* enough to fit *me* in. So, fill them bad boys up and take 'em back to Jersey. Jason's sister has a closet worth of space, so don't try to kill her crib with all your stuff. That ain't cool."

"I know. I'm not. I just wanna get back whatever I leave with her," she said, stuffing her dust covered computer monitor into a large plastic bag that already looked full.

"Yeah, I hope you do," I said, observing her valuable belongings, realizing that a majority of them weren't coming with her as she continued to mishandle the monitor. "Listen, I don't wanna be the bad guy today, Lyd, but you're gonna have to either give your computer to the Salvation Army or leave it here. The call is yours."

"I hate this!" she said, striking the screen. "Look at me. My life is worthless. Look at me!" she screamed, pushing the heavy bag over, causing everything that sat near the top to spill out. I felt her anger. Her grief had become contagious. I lowered my eyes towards my lap and kept folding her sheets.

Another two hours melted away. Lydea's emotions climaxed and fell like a leaf in the wind. She cried. She laughed. She rambled on and on, and then sat there in silence with nothing to say. We remained seated on the room floor and spoke about her past summer months in her dungeon-like room. Not once did she inform me of anything positive taking place there. We grazed the topic of her future and how blank it looked. I gave her hope the best way that I knew how. I stood up from my seated position and stretched. "Whatever the future has in store for you," I told her, "best believe, it won't repeat what you endured while you stayed here. That's for sure."

"Who knows?" she replied in a low spirit.

"I mean, look on the bright side. Once your dad wakes up from his coma, and God will certainly make sure that he does, your pretty face will be the first one that he sees."

"Well, what if I want *his* face to be the first one I see at my graduation next May?"

As Lydea complained, we continued to separate the good clothes from the bad. I sat on the corner of the bed and my mind gradually detached itself from the conversation. My thoughts were set adrift on memory bliss. I began to think back to our first conversation in the library when I received her number. I was elated back then, kicking game to the same girl who I was helping to move out. All those lost hours we spent in the library, flirting and studying, concurrently tickled my thoughts. Those nice warm days when we strolled around campus brought a grin to my face. Every date we ever went on took its sweet time flashing through my head. Lydea's soprano voice, became merely a moving mouth as my daydream clogged my ears to hear her words.

Our trip to New York City remained fresh in my mind. I thought about the incredible time spent during our spring break, and the lazy time together in her dorm room. All of our time spent shopping ran laps in my memory, and even the moments that we shared during the week I left for Atlanta walked down my hall of memories as well.

I reflected on the morning when I left Newport News at 6:30 a.m. to pick her up from campus just so she could attend an extra-credit Criminal Justice group discussion that was held at the Virginia Beach Higher Learning Center at 8 a.m. What a memorable day that was. We left with so much free food that afternoon; we looked like two laughing gluttons. Every laughing moment the two of us experienced as a couple hit me all at once while sitting across from her in the low-lit room, packing her clothes. After mind traveling, I returned from my mental vacation.

"Jay, did you hear me?" Lydea said. "Pass me another plastic bag. My suitcases are full."

"Oh, sorry," I said, passing her a bag. "I thought you said something else."

By this time, it was slightly after 6 p.m. and there was still much left to do. While we worked, she constantly brought up Jason's name. Her doing so reminded me of the lyrics to a hip-hop song by the highly respected Chicagoan artist, Common.

"Yo, Lyd, do you remember those lyrics I printed out for you last semester?" I asked.

"Yeah. A little bit. I remember the song was called 'Ghetto Heaven'. What about it?"

"All this talk about Jason reminds me of those lyrics, that's all. The second verse was about being dependent on God and not some guy you call a friend. Remember now?"

"How could I forget? You highlighted that part."

I watched as my sullen ex-girlfriend continued to pack clothes. She looked so depressed. Was Jesus giving me another opportunity to reveal his love? Did he want me to pray for her right there? Since we were no longer a couple, I became passive and missed my chance to minister to her broken spirit. After the last trash bag was filled, we used her purses and all other small compartments for storage. We both stood to our feet and looked around. All was packed.

We crammed my backseat with six large, black plastic bags as Lydea's motivation to go any further turned into anger. She began hurling the last few bags into my trunk with force, cussing as she did so. I held on to hope, despite the hopelessness. Once my Accord was full, we drove straight to the Salvation Army across town and made our drop off. When we returned to the complex to load up for a second time, we noticed Carla's friends moving in their luggage, ready to consume the available space.

"Dang, girl, you see that. She ain't wastin' no time kickin' you out, is she?" I said, turning off my engine. "That's messed up, yo. At least wait until you're gone. You know?"

"Lydea!" Carla hollered, as we paced towards the front stoop. "Have you spoken with Jason since he left? I need to reach him. He owes me $300 in rent."

"No. Why would he call me?" Lydea sharply replied, striding right through the doorway and up the metal stairs as I trailed close behind.

Shortly after gathering the remaining items from the bedroom, Carla stuck her head in the room and placed her finger over her lips, glaring at me to remain quiet while Lydea faced the closet. Like a professional thief, she took Lydea's cell phone from off the charger by the door. My eyebrows sprung up.

"Jayden, have you seen Jason's phone?" Lydea questioned minutes later. "It was right here."

"Uh, yeah. Your girl, Carla, grabbed it while you were getting your purses," I said, still cleaning up.

"What? Why didn't you say something? I need that phone!"

"I don't know," I said, playing dumb.

"It's the only way I can reach my folks," she said storming out, throwing her small purse at me.

We both stepped into the living room to confront Carla about the phone, as if she were going to give it back. The house was heated and the thermostat had nothing to do with it. Plus, Lydea had just flat out lied about not speaking with Jason when she had that morning. To our favor, Jason's sister knocked on the door at that very moment, ready to help us with the load, but little did she know what she was walking into. Immediately, Lydea pulled her to the side.

"Thanks for coming when you did. Listen, Carla has Jason's phone. She took it when my back was turned. I need it. Can you get it back for me, please? I'll do anything."

"Oh, Lord," Jason's sister sighed, turning around. "Carla!" And that's all she said. I can't explain it, but somehow this straight-faced woman, who looked just like her brother, effortlessly got Carla to return the phone.

Carla cut her eyes in Lydea's direction. "You want your phone? Huh? You want your damn phone?" she said stripping the battery. "There, take it!" she shouted, throwing it towards her feet, stuffing the battery in her back pocket. "Take it and get the hell outta my house. All of y'all. I know Jason called you, you damn liar. He owes me $300!"

Lydea picked up the pieces to her phone and walked away. She cleared the bedroom in a silent fury as I helped with her last few articles. Once we filled the two cars with the remains, I followed Jason's sister back to her townhouse.

"Hey, sorry you had to go through all that back there," I said to Lydea, while I steered. "What's ol' girl's name—Jason's sister? I don't know what to call her."

"I don't know. Who cares?" She shrugged. "Thanks for letting Carla take my phone by the way."

"I said, sorry. And why don't you know her name? You've slept at her house like mad times."

"I mean, I know it but, it's a long name. I can't pronounce it right now, okay? Just don't call her anything."

I looked at Lydea with her arms folded in my passenger seat as if she were joking. "That's dirty. You ain't right."

"*Thank you,*" she said with derision. "I wanna hear you try to say it. Ask her what her name is when we get out."

"Man, I ain't asking that lady nothin'. She won't know my name and I won't know hers. And *you* won't know it either. There."

"That's fine with me. I don't care right now." She flailed her arms. "I see why folks drink. I'm about to lose my mind."

We arrived at Jason's sister's house soon after and worked rapidly. We emptied our vehicles and filled her spare closet with Lydea's possessions. When our mission was finally accomplished, I thanked her and hopped back in my car, still wondering what her name was.

"Hey, what time are we supposed to meet your friend, Arnold, in Hampton again?" I asked merging onto the highway.

"At nine," she said, pulling back her sleeve, glancing at her watch. "We have twenty-two minutes to get there."

"Cool. We should make it on time if traffic allows."

"Can you drive fast for once, please? I really need to meet him at nine."

"Yo, chill. Let me drive. I got this," I said in a relaxed manner, stepping on the gas. "Give him a call," I suggested. "Let 'em know that we're on our way. And if you don't mind me asking, what are we meeting him for? I gotta give the cops a good reason for speeding when I get pulled."

"You're speeding because Arnold's friend has the hookup at a hotel that he works at. So I *really* need to meet him no later than nine."

"Stop playing!" I yelled. "Oh nah! Nah! Not now."

"What?"

"They got me. I spoke too soon. They got me!"

"Who? The cops?" Lydea spun around.

"Yeah. Look at their lights flashing. They're right behind us. Don't turn around!"

"Pull over, boy. How fast were you going?"

"I had just broke eighty," I said, slowing down, pulling onto the shoulder. "That's almost thirty over, Lydea. This ain't good." I shook my head.

The officer parked behind us with his blue lights still pacing. He approached my driver's side. "License and registration," the brawny State patrolman commanded, as I handed them over. "Do you know how fast you were going back there, young man?" he asked me, looking over my ID.

"Yes, officer." I squinted from his bright flashlight.

"Why were you speeding in a work zone, Mr. Rockaway?"

"Well, sir—"

"Officer it was my fault," Lydea cut me short. "I have to meet a friend in less than twenty minutes out in Hampton. It's a life or death situation. He's speeding because I asked him to. I apologize."

The officer bent down and pointed his flashlight at Lydea, sitting in my passenger seat. "Life or death, huh? I'll be right back."

"Oh my goodness, Arnold is gonna kill me," Lydea said, restless, while the officer leisurely walked away. "We're supposed to meet him at nine! He's gonna kill me!"

"Chill. I'm 'bouta get a fat ticket 'cause of you, girl."

"No, you won't. I saw the way the officer looked at me. You'll be fine. We still gotta speed though. I *have* to meet Arnold."

The officer returned shortly after. His flashlight seemed brighter than before. "Life or death, huh?" he said, handing me back my identification. "Mr. Rockaway your record is clean. Keep it that way, young man. The speed limit is fifty-five. No excuses. Have a nice night."

The patrolman walked away, and Lydea and I met eyes, sharing a wide smile. Finally, 17 minutes after the hour, we pulled into the hotel parking lot behind Arnold's jeep. Lydea dashed to his window and tapped. He rolled his window down halfway, and I lowered my music to hear them.

"Yo, what happened to no later than nine o'clock?" he asked in a deep accented voice, looking back at my car.

"I'm sorry we're late," she said, stepping back from his car door, waiting for this heavyset Latino friend of hers to get out. "What did your friend say he could do for me, again?"

"Well, well, I'm sorry you're late, too," he said shutting the door. "Since you and that cat in the whip got here after nine, there's nothin' me or my partna can do. It's too late. I told you no later than nine. You see what my watch says, Lydea? You see that? Sorry is right."

"What do you mean?" she hollered. "Don't make it seem like we're four hours late, Arnold. Your friend can still do something, I'm sure. Anything! Where am I supposed to sleep tonight? Talk to him again." She tugged. "*Please.*"

"He got off at nine!" Arnold lifted his voice. "He left already. I told you, it's too late. You always do this."

Despite his size, she began hitting him in desperation. "No. No!" she yelled. "He can still do something."

Arnold grew irritated and got back in his jeep. "Get off me! You still haven't changed. I hope your boy got your back!" He slammed his door shut and sped off.

This wasn't how the night was supposed to end. Lydea was once again my responsibility and I had to find a place for her to rest her head. Her whirling emotions had already pricked my last nerve, but I was hard-pressed to not react like her friend had. I remained patient and tolerated her multiple moods. I couldn't allow her words of anger to offend me.

We remained parked with my engine running, waiting for our next move. "You know what?" she blurted. "I don't even care anymore. Just drop me off at the stupid station." She plunged forward, attempting to put my gear in drive.

"What? Stop!" I shouted, catching her hand in motion. "Stop talkin' crazy. I ain't leavin' you at no station."

"Do it! I don't care anymore. This way you don't have to see me in the morning. Start driving. Just—just go!" she said enraged, still upset about Arnold leaving the way he did.

I drove away, knowing that the Newport News motels were priced lower than the ones in Hampton. Three stops later, we came across a cheap rate and she paid for a room. I removed her necessities from my car and dropped them off by her bedside. Exhausted from a long day, I said good-bye from a distance, creeping towards my car to leave.

"Jayden, wait," Lydea said, hurrying towards me. She stood directly in front of me and fiddled with her hair. "Hey, um, thanks for everything today," she said in a soft lady-like manner. "This morning, and afternoon, and evening, and all. I really appreciate it."

"Oh, no problem. I'm glad I could help you." I stood tired, inhaling a deep breath. "You straight?"

"No," she replied, with a miserable face, a sad face. "I'm not good at all. My life shouldn't be like this. Do you realize I literally dropped out of school today? The start of my senior year is shot. There's nothing for me in Camden."

"You're taking a semester off, there's a difference. And your father is in Camden. It'll all work out in the end, Lyd. I'm sure the Lord will take care of the both of you. Trust in God's compass. Ask him for guidance and he'll give it to you. You'll be fine."

"Yeah," she said, looking up. "You know I went to church yesterday morning, for the first time in a while, and the pastor spoke that very message."

"You went to service? Wow. How was it?"

"I cried a lot," Lydea grinned. "An altar call was given towards the end, and I actually went up there and gave my heart to Jesus. Can you believe it? I repented so hard, Jayden, for everything. All that you and I have done. All that junk between me and Jason. I mean *everything*. All my sins."

"That's real talk, Lyd."

"Yeah, I know. And I'm sure you won't believe this but, I actually decided to remain abstinent until I get married." She beamed. "You think I can do it?"

"You're gonna laugh...I made the same decision earlier this summer." I chuckled, looking at my beautiful friend. "So, yes, I think you can do it. If I can do it, you can too. It's a daily decision. We just gotta keep our mind on God, ya dig?"

She casually nodded in agreement. "Thanks for being here for me, Jay. I mean it. You have no idea how much I want to thank you."

"You're good. No problem. Really."

"You look tired," Lydea perceived. "I better let you go. It's getting late," she said, stroking the length of her hair as I stood there. "Can I hug you good-bye?"

I stepped towards her with my arms wide open. In the stillness of the night, positioned in a motel parking lot, we held one another with no lust, no temptation, simply pure compassion. The opportunity to spark an old flame was right before us, but that wasn't what she needed from me. "I'll be back in the morning," I added a while later, as she released her grasp. "You need a good night's sleep, Lyd. That's all the both of us really need."

"Thanks for everything, Jay," she said, walking back to her room. "Good night. I'll see you in the morning."

By the time I opened my car door, I heard the sound of the chain being locked to the latch. It was strange how I felt no temptation to follow Lydea into the motel when just months before, I would've been enticed by the opportunity. Oh, how we had grown.

Breakdown

Many questions in my head were answered that day. The number one revelation that I received from God was found in Ecclesiastes 3:1: "*To everything there is a season, and a time to every purpose under heaven.*" Neither one of us could've predicted our closing moments being what they were. She was the most intelligent student I personally knew at NNU and I had to witness her withdraw from school. Her father's loss of consciousness lodged a fork in the road, which made Lydea choose a path to go down. She knew that God had something to do with it all, but she didn't know what. It's funny how seasons in our life play out, would you agree?

Looking back, I regret not introducing Lydea to Jesus like he originally asked me to. She had always acknowledged who Jesus was, but didn't quite understand the carnal and eternal benefits of a personal relationship with him. If there was anything I would've changed from our past, it would not have been the breakups or the heartaches the both of us endured. I would not have even removed Jason from the picture, but what I would have done differently would have been to live up to the high calling of a Christian, by being Christ-like.

~ Work of Art ~

37

The next morning, I must've hit snooze five times. I literally couldn't get out of the bed. I eventually got dressed and prepared myself for an experience that I was grateful to be a part of. I pulled up to the motel and helped Lydea with her luggage. Her attitude was lax. We drove to the Hampton Greyhound in silence. She was speechless and so was I.

The two of us walked through the doors of the station with her obese luggage. She split to the ticket booth, as I sat across from a middle-aged couple that had double the amount of luggage that she had. Lydea received her bus ticket and sat next to me, still quiet. Her body language made it hard to tell if she was willing or unwilling to get on the bus. I had no idea what was spinning through her head. Our morning hour slowly decreased from minutes to seconds as her transportation began boarding.

"Well, it looks like I'd better go," she said with a careless gleam, turning from me, looking at the bus driver.

"Wait, I have something for you." I dug deep into my pocket. "Here. This is for you." I handed her a small wrapped box. "Happy birthday, pretty lady. Open it later, okay?"

"Jay, you remembered." She looked up with falling tears. "Why are you so good to me, after all I've done?"

I embraced her, long and firm. The last call for her departure was heard. "God is good to you," I whispered in her ear. She reluctantly let me go, and then grabbed her carry-on bag. I watched her climb onto the bus and sit down, thinking out loud, *Oh my goodness, Lord, was this how you planned it from the day we met? Is this the end of our story?*

The moment her bus pulled away, our eyes locked. Lydea pressed her hand against the tinted glass window. I stood right where she had left me and waved back. At that very moment, I blinked and time froze. I fell into a trance. The image that God painted on my canvas was Lydea and I waving good-bye to one another on a gorgeous summer morning. It took the Lord almost a full year to sort the colors of his work of art, just so I could cherish the mental picture that was created. It was beyond reality. Deeper than any dream. She rode away as I stood far off. It was as if the story of our relationship had already been written.

That day, God proved himself to be the painter, author, and weatherman of my life. It's no coincidence that Lydea and I made "Can You Stand the Rain," by the legendary R&B group, New Edition, our favorite song. Thank you, Lord for the weather you gave. I will call it Liquid Sunshine.

Breakdown

To the individual reading my written words, remember this: regardless of your stormy weather, the sun will shine again. When God closes one door, he will open another; when he ends one season, best believe another has already begun; when God completes a painting in your life, realize that others are in progress. Ask him to open your eyes and you will see them.

Can you relate to Lydea's character? Intelligent with an unclear future, fractured heart, abused life, and an unstable family? I hope Lydea personally knows the Lord after all he has done for her. She ended a thunderstorm-like season and simultaneously started a new one. A new day, purpose, and lifestyle awaited her in New Jersey. I pray that she and her father have reconciled by now. I believe she made the right choice to put her father before herself. How many of you would have done the same?

Can you relate to Jason's character? A confused drug-using, abusive street soldier from a broken home? Many individuals have either heard of or know someone just like him. I can't personally relate to his fatherless childhood. I didn't grow up in the inner city with a single mother and siblings. I can't familiarize myself with that half of his life, but I do have a desire to be complete, just like he does. We both share the same pursuit of identity. I pray that he has found it. There is so much hope for that young man.

Can you relate to my character, Jayden? He had a decent home, a bright future, and was a church-going hypocrite who struggled to control his flesh. Yes, he was very much a hypocrite. He wanted to do right, instead he did wrong. He practiced sin behind closed doors while Jesus watched from above. His actions were motivated by disobedience, but it's humbling to know that he has been forgiven. His past sins were separated as far as the east is from the west. I believe, of the three main characters, if Jayden hadn't turned from his sins, his punishment would've been far greater than the others on judgment day because he knew what to flee from. But thank God the blood of Christ has already surmounted our sins and all that is required is our repentance.

I encourage those who confess Jesus as their Lord and Savior to cease all hypocrisy. Do away with your two-facedness. Learn how to walk in the spirit and not in the flesh. When searching for the will of God, remember these words: it starts and ends with obeying the commandments throughout the B.I.B.L.E. These are our Basic Instructions Before Leaving Earth. Obeying the Father with a pure motive has enough power to put a smile on Jesus' face, from ear-to-ear. Obedience is how we love him! Religion won't cut it. We can't work our way into heaven. That's insane. Being a good person is vanity if Jesus isn't your reason for doing so. Take regard, to fear the Lord is wisdom and to avoid evil is understanding. So then don't be foolish, but know what the will of the Lord is. Think it over. God will make it all plain.

It's no wonder that Pastor John Bevere, an anointed messenger of God, said in his *Driven by Eternity* DVD series that the five manifestations of fearing God are to: obey instantly, obey when you don't see a benefit, obey even when it hurts, obey until completion, and obey even when it doesn't make sense.

I love scripture. He who has an ear, let him hear what the Holy Spirit has revealed to me. God's will and purpose for our lives go-arm in-arm, like a bride and groom. *"So do not throw away your confidence; it will be richly rewarded. You need to persevere so that after you have done the will of God you will receive what he has promised"* (Hebrews 10:35-36 NIV). In order to know what God has promised, we must know what the Bible says. Scripture is filled with guarantees. I challenge you to study it.

Jesus' obedience to his Father, our heavenly Father, fulfilled his purpose, even unto his death and resurrection. Because Jesus *died* in obedience for me, I'd be honored to *live* in obedience for him.

~ Prayer of Salvation ~

If you do not know Jesus Christ as your personal Lord and Savior, I motivate and encourage you to engage the number one, most important relationship you will ever have. Everything else in this life is vanity. If you choose to make this vocal commitment, wholeheartedly read the following prayer out loud to the Lord:

Heavenly Father, I recognize and admit that I am a sinner. Please forgive me of my sinful and disobedient ways. Jesus, wash me clean with your precious blood.

Without further delay, I turn from my selfish ways and walk in full spiritual, physical, and emotional obedience, as you command of me. Jesus, I believe in my heart, you lived, died, and defeated death through your resurrection, just so I could be saved.

Bless me now and forevermore with the power and wisdom of the Holy Spirit as I receive my salvation.

In Jesus' name,

Amen!

Printed in the United States
153573LV00003B/3/P